A DAY IN
GOD'S COUNTRY

A Shore Story

George Kotarides, Jr.

Warehouse One, LLC

A DAY IN GOD'S COUNTRY: A SHORE STORY

Copyright © 2007 by George Kotarides, Jr.

Warehouse One, LLC
155 Cypress Street
Fort Bragg, CA 95437
(800) 773-7782
E-mail: georgekotarides@aol.com

Book and cover design by Mike Brechner / Cypress House
Cover photo by Stacy Kotarides

PUBLISHER'S CATALOGING-IN-PUBLICATION DATA

Kotarides, George.
    A day in God's country : a shore story / George Kotarides, Jr. -- 1st ed. -- Norfolk, VA : Warehouse One, 2007.
        p. ; cm.
    ISBN-13: 978-0-9791101-5-3
    ISBN-10: 0-9791101-5-7
    1. Surfing--Fiction. 2. Adventure stories. 3. Young adult fiction.
I. Title.
    PS3611.O837 D39 2007
    813.6--dc22 0705

PRINTED IN THE USA
9 8 7 6 5 4 3 2 1

In loving memory of Gemma and Otis Williams

For Mom and Dad

1. A Sunny Day Interrupted

It was a calm August morning. The flat sands had just started to warm from the rays of the rising sun. Peaceful waters lazily lapped the shoreline freshly dotted with sun worshipers eager to soak up every drop of the magnificent day. Children frolicked on rafts while parents positioned beach chairs for optimum tanning or people watching, digging their pale toes into the white sand. As the day wore on, these countless fine grains would bake to an unbearable intensity, requiring flip-flops to protect naked feet. Such steamy yet perfectly placid days often grace the Mid-Atlantic, luring millions of hard-working Americans to its beaches where clusters of development known as resorts accommodate and entertain. Some call them tourist traps. One such place is Virginia Beach, an excellent trap indeed.

Something odd was unfolding in the heating sand. People came from up and down the beach to witness a strange spectacle. The assembled travelers, residents, and emergency personnel were gathered around a figure dressed in white, a boy, who sat at the center of an ever-growing mass. He sat motionless, downcast, facing the glistening sea. Few details were known, except that a disturbed boy, a solitary sentinel in the center of a congregation, had the attention of a lot of people, and more were coming.

"The kid just lost it," the buff lifeguard in red trunks stated matter-of-factly to the teenage girl in a red one-piece suit that distinguished her as a beach employee. She gazed up at him on his perch.

"What do you think happened?" she asked. The blue-eyed chair and umbrella attendant spoke quickly and with a West Coast lilt, as she flipped her long, blond hair over her shoulder, and rotated her neck simultaneously.

"I dunno, but he's caused a huge mess."

"Do you think they'll put him away?" she asked with an extra lilt on "away."

"They should. What he said ... it's just weird. I've never heard anything like it."

"He sounds like one of those kids who goes nuts and plants bombs or shoots up a school," she said with a knowing air.

While reporters on the boardwalk interviewed bystanders, the lifeguard and beach attendant continued whispering. Several reporters made their way through the crowd and surrounded the boy.

"Did you hear anything he said?" said one reporter to the pixie-like chair attendant. She just looked at the scribe, hesitating long enough for someone else to answer.

"I heard him shout across the beach that buildings will fall," interjected one bystander. This caused the crowd to buzz like an audience before the curtain rises for a performance.

The reporter turned away and addressed the gathering. "Does anybody know his name?" she asked, pad and pencil in hand.

Nobody answered.

Then the police captain arrived. He pushed through the throng and headed down to the beach to where the boy was sitting. Sweat lines traced his chiseled black face.

A reporter with a Channel 10 microphone and a cameraman asked the captain as he passed, "Was the boy receiving psychiatric treatment? Is he from a mental hospital?"

"Can't answer yet."

"Captain, do we know this boy's name?" hollered another reporter, who shoved a Channel 3 mic at him.

The officer turned and called back over his shoulder as he hurried on, "We don't know much yet."

A young reporter in a business suit, her cameraman locked in at the ready, probed, "Captain, where is this boy's family? Can you comment on the things he's been saying?"

"Is this a bomb scare? Why haven't you evacuated any buildings?" hollered an unseen male voice from the back of the crowd, unsettling many onlookers.

"Have to go now," the grim-faced captain said dismissively as he continued across the sand.

Police and beach patrol kept the curious at a distance from the boy, who remained cross-legged, looking out over the water. A tear fell onto the sand.

The captain looked at the weeping boy, then turned away and reached for his radio. "We need a chaplain and a psychiatrist down here. We have a boy, around twelve or thirteen, apparently threatening to blow up buildings."

The captain then turned, approached the boy, and squatted down in front of him.

"Young man, I'm Captain Wallace. I want to help you. What's your name?"

There was no answer. In his mid-thirties, Wallace had a master's degree in sociology from the nearby university, along with prior experience as a social worker. Over the years, he had learned how to talk people out of doing stupid things.

"It's hot. Do you want some water?" Wallace looked over to the cops nearby and ordered, "Get me some water for this boy!" Then he continued, "Son, what is your name?"

The boy looked at him sadly and answered, "My name doesn't matter."

This was a new one to the captain. "I can't help you if you don't

3

tell me your name."

"I don't need help!" he sobbed. "The others need help! They are going to die!"

"Who are these other people?"

"The people in that building." The boy turned and pointed to a high-rise hotel. He caught his breath. Tears now streamed down his face. "But you won't listen...nobody will listen, and it's too late."

"Did you plant a bomb in that building? Did somebody plant a bomb?"

"No!" The boy put his head in his hands and tugged at his wavy brown hair.

"If you didn't put a bomb in that building, son, and you know of no one who did, then how do you know people in that building are going to die?"

The boy sobbed uncontrollably as he turned to the officer and choked out in a half-cry, half-whisper, "God told me."

"What?"

The boy turned and exclaimed pleadingly, "God told me!"

Some of the nearby police officers, within earshot, looked at one another and rolled their eyes.

"This is getting us nowhere, son. You're not making sense here. Please tell me what—"

"Let me talk with him," a large, dark figure interrupted.

The captain paused a moment as Chaplain Matthew O'Leary walked up to the boy, who still sat weeping.

"Alone, please."

"Sure. No problem." The captain walked back to the growing crowd of policemen, lifeguards, beach attendants, and onlookers. It now seemed like the chaplain was more qualified to deal with a boy who thinks he hears God.

As people speculated about what they thought was happening, an intent O'Leary listened quietly as the boy spoke. While the minutes passed, the crowd got more restless; rumors circulated. About ten yards from the boy and the chaplain, the captain gestured for everyone to stay back and called on his radio for assistance. In seconds, several uniformed cops on ATVs motored onto the scene, hopped off their four-wheelers, and kept the crowd at bay. Then, an officer, who pointed in the direction of the boardwalk, called Captain Wallace away from his crowd-control duties. "Excuse me, sir. The psychiatrist is here." Wallace turned.

Wearing a dark suit and tie, thirty-four-year-old prison psychiatrist Dr. Thomas Schmidt, tall and thin with stooped shoulders, walked across the beach with an air of confidence. He specialized in prison counseling and medicating society's dregs: juvenile delinquents, child molesters, and drug dealers.

"So, what has the boy said?" the doctor asked the captain, the slightest air of condescension in his tone.

"He's been talking about being sent by God; sounds like a religious wacko."

"What exactly has he said, Captain? I need specifics."

"Like I said, he told me he was sent by God, sort of like a messenger, I guess … and that buildings are going to blow up … well, specifically, that building there," pointing at the twenty-story hotel behind them, just beyond the beach.

"How long has he been sitting there?" asked Schmidt after a contemplative pause.

"Uh, I don't know. We've been here thirty minutes or so, and he hasn't moved much."

"Who's been talking with him?"

"Well, I talked with him awhile, and the chaplain is speaking to him now. He's been with the boy for about fifteen minutes. Earlier, the lifeguard here heard him talking 'woo-woo' stuff. He radioed his superior who in turn contacted us. So now, here we all are. Nice way to spend a sunny morning, watching some kid act crazy," he finished with a shake of his head.

"Could you get the chaplain for me?" Dr. Schmidt requested.

5

The captain walked over to O'Leary, who wore a black shirt underneath his black police-issue chaplain's uniform. Perspiration ran down his chubby, pale face, and tears filled his eyes. His stringy brown hair lay matted to his forehead. When Wallace approached, O'Leary turned from the boy and looked up, pushing up the wired spectacles that had slid down his nose.

Wallace leaned down and quietly informed the chaplain, "We've called in a psychiatrist. He's just over here. Would you come with—?"

"A psychiatrist?" questioned O'Leary, swiping at tears that poured down his cheeks. Whatever the boy had told him had greatly affected him. He collected himself, then added, "He seems quite troubled, I know, but I'm not sure a psychiatrist is going to—"

Wallace cut him off. "I need you to fill the psychiatrist in on what the boy's been saying to you," he said with finality as he helped O'Leary out of his crouch. Wallace didn't want to hear the religious man's opinion of whether the boy needed a shrink. That decision would be his. After all, he was the man in charge. And as soon as he got a handle on exactly what was happening with that building behind them, the boy would be arrested. Right now, all he wanted was information about a bomb.

They walked over to Dr. Schmidt, who stood twenty yards up the beach. The sunlight blinded O'Leary; he shaded his eyes to put a face on the silhouette before him. The captain made introductions as Schmidt gazed blankly at the somber clergyman. Wallace began, "Due to the nature of what he's been saying, we called the chaplain here to, well, to relate to— I mean, to reason with him." Dr. Schmidt coolly offered his hand. O'Leary shook it and then stood silently.

"My name is Dr. Thomas Schmidt. I am a psychiatrist," he started with an authoritative air. "Can you tell me what the boy has said, what he wants?"

O'Leary seemed at a loss for words.

"You've spoken to him," Schmidt said. "Did he tell you his name?"

When O'Leary still did not respond, a frustrated Schmidt shook his head and looked to Wallace.

"Chaplain O'Leary?" prompted the captain.

The chaplain sighed and met the psychiatrist's gaze. "You can't help this boy. It's clear he's going through something very profound. You don't know what you're dealing with," he said gruffly.

After the psychiatrist had questioned the boy, been briefed by various authorities, and had listened to the murmurs of the crowd, he took a pad out of his pocket and reviewed his notes. "Well, by all accounts he certainly seems to suffer from some kind of grandiose notions, to say the least. He could be delusional, perhaps schizophrenic."

Nearby, an eavesdropping officer interjected, "And he says we're all out to get him. Guess he's paranoid, too."

Wallace turned to the cop and pointed his finger at him in frustration. "Officer, pipe down!" Turning back to Schmidt, he explained, "That's what some bystander said. We really don't know exactly what's going on. People here say he's threatened to bomb that building over there." Wallace pointed over his shoulder with his thumb. "But when I talked with him, he said he didn't plant a bomb. He just keeps saying that people are going to die."

The chaplain lowered his head and closed his eyes tightly.

Wallace wondered if the boy might already be in treatment somewhere. He wanted to give his folks a chance to pick him up before the police took him into custody. For almost an hour they searched for the boy's parents, using the resort area's public address system. Between sets of elevator-style reggae music, lost child announcements were broadcast on speakers that lined the concrete boardwalk and the congested pedestrian shopping and entertainment area just beyond it. The announcements described a boy around twelve or thirteen, with brown hair, blue eyes, about five feet two inches tall, 120 pounds, and wearing a BEACHES ARE FOR LOVERS T-shirt. But there was no response.

People strolling along the boardwalk and beach continued to stop to see what was happening and to take pictures of an enormous statue of a trident-wielding Neptune that stood in the nearby grassy patch of land known as Sunnyside Park. At present, the forty-foot god of the sea seemed to preside over the events unfolding on the beach. On the boardwalk, a contingent of reporters, official personnel, and news crews induced more observers to stop and gawk, many of whom hoped to be interviewed or get their faces on TV.

Then, without warning, the boy spoke again. Wide-eyed, he turned to the two nearest officers and said, "I know this sounds crazy to you, but a voice tells me I am a messenger sent here to tell you what you don't want to hear. The voice says, 'Today there will be death and destruction. Now your eyes are open, but still you see nothing.'"

The officers looked at each other incredulously. One whispered, "Did you hear that? Where'd he get that crazy stuff?"

The other turned to his buddy, shielded his mouth with the back of his hand, and added with a smirk, "I'll bet his parents are the ones messin' this kid up — probably religious freaks or part of some cult."

Then somebody in the crowd behind the officers called out, "Yeah, sure kid, where'd you hear that one!"

The boy dropped his head into his hands and said with resignation, "I just told you."

2. The Arrival

THE SKY WAS CAROLINA BLUE against an azure sea. A string of pelicans skirted the tops of knee-high, glassy rollers. The awkward birds undulated just above the waves, which crested and fell, disappearing into the sand. It was a quiet morning, save for the cry of a lone seagull gliding high overhead and the background music of a steady parade of waves.

This was one of those flat, unsurfable days when Francis would look out his window and think. He and his mother, Anne, had lived in a two-story North Beach cottage in Virginia Beach since he was born. Now fourteen, and with a pudgy belly, he still spoke with a child's voice. As Francis gazed at the horizon, he thought of mornings when the surf was up. Before his mom awakened, he'd sneak out solo at first light and paddle out to the break. There, he'd sit and wait for the perfect ride, along with resident dolphins that seemed to arrive from nowhere to surf with him. Sometimes, on really good days, that marvelous wave would appear in a matter of seconds. After the ride, as he turned over the back of the wave, he'd throw his arms in the air, drop to his chest, and paddle out again to catch an even more perfect swell. But on this day he could only imagine, as his mother prepared breakfast downstairs.

"When's it going to happen?" he muttered while brushing his teeth. Would he ever reach puberty? Of the fifty boys in his freshman class, it seemed that he and maybe one other kid were stuck in developmental neutral. He knew it would happen, but in the back of his mind he wondered if he was some sort of biological anomaly. Francis went to First Colony Preparatory Academy, an elite private school with a storied history of graduating prominent doctors, lawyers, politicians, and businessmen since colonial times. Over the years it had been called different names, such as the County Prep School, and then, in the late 1800s, Princess Anne County Prep School. In 1963, rural Princess Anne County and the small city on the shores of the Atlantic, Virginia Beach, merged, creating Virginia's largest and most populous city. The next year, the school was named First Colony Preparatory Academy, or, as it was called with an air of mock snobbery that wasn't so mock, The Academy, for short. Upon graduating, kids were expected to go to college. Invariably, everyone did.

The sprawling campus featured state-of-the-art facilities, including an acoustically perfect 500-seat auditorium, replete with balconies and private boxes for dignitaries and high-ranking faculty, a first-class music and fine arts building, dedicated laboratories for each of the sciences, several athletic fields with stadium lights, two gymnasiums, an Olympic swimming pool, a massive library, and a modern media center. Parents would drive their kids to school in huge SUVs and 500 Class Mercedeses on their way to tennis with the girls at the country club or to a day's work billing $300 an hour as lawyers while golfing with politico/developer chums. Buildings often rose and fell at the whim of these golf foursomes, who had been anointed by city planners to manifest the vision and, of course, best interests of the "community at large."

"Are you coming down to eat breakfast, sweetie?" Francis' mother called up the stairs. "Your eggs are getting cold, and you're late for the bus. Looks like I'm going to drive you again. And you know

10

your dad's coming today. I have to pick him up at the airport."

Francis called down, "I'm coming, Mom."

He brushed his teeth thoroughly, as his father had taught him when he was very little. The last time Francis had seen his father was four years ago. Disappointment invaded his mind as he tied his shoes, for Francis knew it was just another trip his father managed to fit into his busy schedule. Over the past ten years, his father had visited seldom, each time promising to call and visit more. As the years wore on, it had stopped seeming like his father talking on the other end and started seeming like just a man he used to know.

Nonetheless, Francis was usually able to put aside his disappointment and genuinely look forward to seeing his dad, who always had stories to tell about the waves in California or the storms he'd surfed when he was a kid. But his infrequent visits lasted only a week or so, not long enough for any real bond to form. When he left, it was always too soon. And he always stayed away too long.

≈

The turbulent cross-country flight from San Diego to Atlanta was miserable. To pass the time, Peter Kahne ruminated about his investments as he sipped another Irish whiskey from the clear plastic cup. Sure, Templeton Foreign Investment was up 48 percent, S&P 500 Index Fund up 30 percent, T. Rowe Price Mid-cap Value Fund up 73 percent, and the little dollar gold-mining stock he'd bought 15,000 shares of last year at 93 cents had struck a vein and was at $57.50. He was making a killing.

Forty-five-year-old Peter looked out the window and stared blankly at the clouds. Despite the bucks Peter raked in, he lived simply in a small condo in San Diego. His friends were bartenders, politicians, and the occasional prolonged one-night stand that would last a few weeks. Middle-aged, chasing young skirts, and living 3,000 miles away from his boy and what used to be his wife and home, he needed another drink.

Down the aisle he spied flight attendant Debbie. Beneath her company-issue blue uniform hose, he could just make out the silhouette of a nice pair of legs, thin ankles, and defined calves, the kind he'd cased since high school at The Academy. On the other hand, the woman next to him was grossly overweight. A few more pounds, he pondered, shaking his head, and she wouldn't be able to fly — too fat for a plane seat. Little Ms. Debbie walked by again. Peter was parched.

"Oh, miss … ma'am," he called out.

"Yes, sir. How may I help you?" she asked politely, but with a tight smile.

"I'd like a Jameson on the rocks, please, and some bottled water."

"Would you like ice for your water, sir?"

"No, thank you," he replied with a sigh, thinking about her legs and the chemicals they put in water that ended up as ice. "Maybe we could get together for a lobster dinner sometime?"

The flight attendant laughed and said something about a boyfriend. Then Peter noticed that the fat woman next to him seemed bothered by all the chatter. She issued a loud sigh, interpretable as "Be quiet, jerk! Can't you see I'm reading the *National Enquirer?*"

How does a person let herself go like that? Peter wondered.

The flight attendant returned with the whiskey and water. Peter leered. She smiled again, briefly, showing a few crow's-feet and slightly crooked teeth. Peter smiled back as she set the miniature bottle and cup of ice down on his tray. He handed her back the ice and paid her five dollars, then looked up at her with blue eyes and the cool rugged handsomeness of a Marlboro model. "Keep the change, sweetheart."

Debbie turned. "Your whiskey costs five dollars, sir." Taking a deep breath, she herself joined the irritated fat lady's club.

But Peter didn't care about his little faux pas. Debbie reminded him of his latest in a long string of girlfriends, a young secretary who looked good in the front office of a law firm, but knew little or nothing about the law, and typed twenty-five words a minute with countless mistakes. Her name didn't matter. Peter thought about her body, her surgically enhanced breasts. She wasn't going to let age win.

After his third Jameson and gazing out the window at the passing clouds, he was asleep, waking up when the wheels touched down in Atlanta. Following a one-hour layover and a short flight, he would soon arrive at Norfolk International Airport and his ex-life.

Anne reminisced as she waited at the baggage claim. She was forty-six and still in love with her ex-husband.

They had met at a fraternity party at the College of William and Mary twenty-six years ago, when Anne Hallstead was a junior and Peter a sophomore. She came from Norfolk and he from Virginia Beach, each with elite, gentrified roots that traced back to the *Mayflower.*

Anne's father, Mitch, was a renowned orthopedist who worked on the elbows and arms of aspiring pitchers. He had even pioneered procedures that ended up being used in surgeries on the top professionals. He and Anne's mother, Lynn, lived in a mansion on the Elizabeth River in Norfolk.

Peter's parents were bluebloods through and through. As members of the prestigious Princess Anne Country Club, they rubbed elbows with upper-crust socialites and power brokers. Rufus, Peter's dad, ate, drank, and slept politics—especially drank. A single-malt scotch man, Rufus' abilities lay in his proficiency at raising money. Politicians who wanted to be elected and entrepreneurs who wanted capital to start up their ventures would call on him for his services. There was none better than Rufus Kahne at getting into the pockets of rich people with nothing better to do than throw their money at things that would make them richer.

Peter's mom, Sally, was an elegant, well-educated woman who knew how to throw parties and entertain. She was also a member of numerous clubs, charities, and civic organizations. The Sally and Rufus team worked. Money poured in, paying for a sprawling eight-bedroom waterfront ranch with a swimming pool and tennis courts in the upscale neighborhood of Bay Colony. If you lived in Bay Colony, you were in the spot. But the grandness of success, popularity, and power concealed a quiet distance between the pair. Sally spent most of her days, when she wasn't attending high-brow functions or preparing the perfect meal for six guests with a combined net worth of $100 million, poring over self-help books on love and intimacy at the nearby Edgar Cayce Center for Research and Enlightenment. Rufus found his peace and enlightenment at the bottom of a glass of twenty-year-old Macallan single malt. Perhaps Peter's little subconscious rebellion was choosing Irish whiskey over scotch.

When Anne graduated, a year before Peter, they were married. She got a job as a pharmaceutical representative. He continued college and earned a degree in political science.

When he graduated, they moved to Virginia Beach and, with the help of their parents, bought a spacious beachfront home in North Beach. The enviable trappings of success soon followed. Peter, aided by having his father's last name, got a job fundraising for the state's largest museum, quickly moving up the ladder to the position of executive director. On weekends he surfed. Anne socialized with the other surf widows. They joined a popular gym, took yoga classes, supported worthy causes, and partied late, often with the aid of a certain white powder in vogue at the time with people in three-story oceanfront mansions. Life was going well, and influential people liked them. With the support of the social elite, Peter decided to run for city council, but lost in a close race, despite his father's support and raising twice the money his opponent did. Unfazed, Peter got used to hobnobbing with the oceanfront party crowd. He stayed out late with his buddies and wanna-be-taken-care-of-by-a-guy-with-a-thick-wallet women, often staggering in the front door to a cold wife and a sleeping Francis.

14

This was Peter's third visit since the divorce, and he looked forward to seeing his old friends and spending a few weeks with Francis. He had taken a leave of absence from his job, and, in the back of his mind, thought of looking for a house on the East Coast, maybe even his hometown. At the moment, he lived off his investments. Jokingly, he would say, especially to women he found attractive, that he was semi-retired, had one foot in the grave, and was independently wealthy. They would laugh, cross their legs in his direction, and order more drinks. As a coup de grace, Peter would dazzle these ladies with the knowledge of wine he'd acquired after ten years in California and the means to order a fat $100 California Cabernet, holding the glass to the dim light, swirling adeptly, and swishing for just the right flavor notes. More than a few times this shtick had gotten him at least a one-nighter.

Anne tried not to look forward to Peter's arrival, but her heartbeat quickened as she applied more lipstick and checked herself in her compact mirror. She wore a tight pair of black slacks with a delicate, white silk blouse. *Not bad for an old lady,* she thought, noticing a few wrinkles, but remembering her firm, athletic body. *Peter will like what he sees.*

While Anne waited, she wondered if her heart would jump like it always had when she saw him after a long time. No matter how much she prepared herself, she couldn't shake this, so she paced back and forth. She told herself what a jerk he was, and reminded herself of horrible things he had done while they were married.

A year or so after they were wed, he had shacked up with Tess, a barely legal blond who made it into *Penthouse* magazine a few years later for screwing around with the governor. Anne found out about the tryst when she and Peter were in line for a VIP table at Il Giardino, a popular resort restaurant. The young couple in front of them knew the gossipy blond. Not realizing Peter and Anne were behind them, the young lady proceeded to recount intimate details of Tess' affair with Peter.

After screaming, "You SOB!" and slapping her wayward husband, Anne ran out of the restaurant and down the street, catching a cab to a girlfriend's apartment. A flood of tears later, Anne returned home to a remorseful Peter. Then there were less dramatic, less public lipstick-on-the-collar episodes. Eventually Peter got smart and stopped wearing white shirts out to the bars, but not even dark shirts could hide home-wrecker perfumes.

Finally, a tanned, trim, and sun-bleached-blond Peter glided down the escalator. He looked younger and more handsome than ever in his designer jeans and black Perry Ellis mock T-shirt, like he had stepped out of the pages of *GQ*. As he approached, Anne stood almost motionless, but couldn't hide her broad smile. For a moment, they surveyed one another, each noticing that age had done its subtle cosmetic work on the other. They leaned toward one another and hugged, hips apart, then retrieved Peter's bags.

They made small talk on their way to the car. Anne filled Peter in on Francis' good grades and the surfing exploits that she knew about; however, there wasn't much catching up about each other on the awkward drive to the beach house they'd built together twenty years ago. Anne really didn't want to hear about Peter's escapades.

During the long silences, Anne remembered how they had grown more and more distant during the last five years of their marriage. Maybe one too many nights with Peter reeking of liquor and some bimbo's perfume had something to do with it, but it wasn't that simple for her. To try to sort things out, to try to move on, she had joined a workshop on relationships called "Communication for Life." She went to church, read all the *Chicken Soup* books, and even took Anthony Robbins seminars. She was still searching for answers.

They pulled up to the house, and Peter grabbed his bags out of the trunk.

"I'll pick up Francis at school. We'll meet you at the house at four, if that's okay. How 'bout if Francis and I catch some surf?"

"Sure," Anne muttered. "Sure, whatever you want. It's your time together." Although she would never admit it, she resented him intruding on her and Francis.

It was midmorning. Peter carried his bags to the guestroom over the garage, which was full of family pictures and memorabilia from their vacations. The futon was pulled out and made up with white sheets and a comforter bearing the First Colony Preparatory Academy logo. Francis' room was two doors down the hall. Peter rolled his suitcase to the foot of the futon and sat down. The sun beamed brightly through the window.

Peter took a deep breath and slapped his knees. He had nothing but time and the prospect of catching up with old friends, and maybe a few new ones. *But first, I'm going to catch some rays,* he thought as he climbed into his trunks, sneaking an admiring glance in the full-length mirror at abs that were now down from a six-pack to a four-pack. Several hours remained until The Academy school day ended, plenty of time to amplify his California tan before picking up Francis.

3. No More Teachers

An air of collective excitement comes over a student body at the end of the school year. The fun and freedoms of summer — surf, ball games, camps, or just hanging out with friends — awaited the 1,247 students of First Colony Prep, where Francis had been an honor student since the first grade. Now, he looked forward to his own little summer heaven: the long days where surfing, thinking about surfing, or talking about surfing took the place of geometry and all other things scholastic. But geometry was okay with Francis for the moment because the prettiest girl in the middle school sat in the row next to him. She reminded him of that wave he dreamed of, smooth and mysteriously formed. Francis sat, floating, and watched her out of the corner of his eye.

"A squared plus B squared equals … anyone?" asked Mrs. Bundy, who had taught geometry at The Academy for thirty years. In all that time, the now elderly teacher had worn the same four pantsuit outfits in red and navy blue, or so it seemed. She would mix them to try to create different looks, but they all looked alike. She wore no adornments or perfume of any kind, and occasionally, after a long day of teaching and writing formulas on the blackboard, it became noticeable that she didn't use deodorant, either.

When no one answered, as if she knew he was daydreaming, Mrs. Bundy turned and asked, "Francis?"

Startled, Francis hesitated.

"Yes, Francis?" she encouraged.

"C squared," Francis answered softly. He quickly glanced next to him, then looked down at his desk. The girl smiled, twirled her hair, and looked away. Her name was Summer.

"Thank you, Francis." Mrs. Bundy liked the quiet and well-mannered youth.

"Now, ladies and gentlemen, on your final exam you will be tested on finding the area of different triangles, circles, and rectangles, plus everything else you learned this year. The exam is cumulative. Know all your formulas; there will also be a section on word problems, and don't forget parabolas!" she said, raising her voice as the bell rang.

Francis got up and looked over to Summer. At that moment, as she turned to him, he looked away, the embarrassment of being a late bloomer almost overwhelming him. Nonetheless, he peeked at Summer again, and his heart leaped, then sank all at once into reality. She was out of his league.

The nearness of summer vacation, combined with The Academy being the antithesis of summer's carefree days, caused classes to drag mercilessly. Finally, the last bell rang, signaling time for PE and then the end of the day. Francis trudged toward the locker room, a daily destination he anticipated with dread. On the way, he usually lingered around the halls or along the walkways and talked to a few friends about whatever kids talk about. If he was lucky, he stood a decent chance of seeing Summer.

As Francis was leaving the middle school building, he felt a gentle tap on his shoulder. He turned. Summer's sweet smile greeted him. His stomach flipped.

They talked awhile about school and Bundy's class and what they were going to do over the summer. Then Summer said, "Hey

Francis, me and some friends are going to the movies and out for pizza. Do you wanna go?"

His heart pounded as he nodded. Summer continued, "Dad's driving us. We could pick you up at seven o'clock if you want. We'll eat pizza at Mike's and then catch a movie."

"Okay– yeah– sure," Francis stuttered, as he backpedaled through the door to the gym. Then he said more confidently, "That'd be great. See you later, Summer."

His glee, however, was tempered by the impending gym class and a locker room full of boys becoming men while he remained stuck in the physiological twilight zone of childhood. So, both agonized and ecstatic, he shuffled toward the locker-room, noticing that he was sweating above his lip and under his bare armpits. He opened the door. The familiar clanking of steel lockers and the smell of adolescent mildew filled the air. Standing in front of his locker, he gathered himself for the quick change at which he had become a master. Then, while removing his shirt, Francis felt another hand on his shoulder. This one was much heavier, as it squeezed twice quickly. The hair on his neck stood straight. It was John.

"What's up, man?" John said with a deep voice as he removed his shirt and pants.

Francis wanted to crawl into his locker. John Constantinides was everything Francis wasn't. Francis had sun-streaked brown hair that hung slightly in his face and touched the back of his collar; John's was black, curly, and cut short. Almost six feet tall, he towered over Francis. Francis' skin and belly were soft. John shaved and was lean and hard with a ripped abdomen. About all they had in common was that they had ridden the same school bus since elementary school and had grown up surfing the same North Beach break.

"Not much. Uh, my dad's coming for a visit today," Francis replied.

"That's cool," replied John as he took off his boxers, prompting Francis to turn away to go to the bathroom — to a stall. When he returned after five minutes of strategic urination, John had dressed and was on his way out the locker room door. Francis kept on his briefs, put on his gym shorts and T-shirt, and made his way to the field with the other boys dressed in phys-ed gray.

Francis sat on a bench, waiting in the warm sun for the other kids and the PE instructor to arrive. He wondered how he would tell his dad about his date with Summer, which conflicted with Peter's first night seeing Francis. The simple truth was, the man who'd left Francis for another life and West Coast ladies would understand more than anyone.

An hour and a half later, Peter pulled in to campus. He had spent the day tanning on the beach, hydrating with Coors Light, and admiring the sights — mostly string bikinis. He found a parking space and daydreamed. "Aqualung" played on the classic rock station as he nodded off, sapped from the sun and a full day of "eyeing little girls with bad intent." Then Francis appeared in front of him and walked around to the passenger side.

"Hi, Dad," Francis said as he opened the door. The bikinis evaporated.

"Hey there, buddy!" Peter hugged his son quickly. "Man, you've grown," he lied. "So, how's school going?"

"Fine," Francis answered, uncomfortable with the beginnings of a forced conversation. Then he regrouped and announced triumphantly, "The prettiest girl in school asked me out for a date. I mean, it's with friends, but she asked me!"

"That's really great. What's her name?" Peter was proud and interested. Now they could talk about girls together — good bonding.

Francis told Peter all about Summer: her dazzling eyes; her flowing, sun-drenched hair; that indescribably delicate citrus aroma she always seemed to have; and most of all, that she liked him. Remembering the last time he'd felt that way, many years ago, Peter realized his boy was in love. Then he smiled and asked, "So, how's your mom?" Francis had to search for what to say.

"She's fine, I guess."

Peter was quiet for a moment. Anne still looked good, he thought, recalling their past lovemaking. The silly notion crossed his mind of what it would be like now. Then he changed to an easier subject. "Checked out the surf already. It's a little flat, but do you wanna go anyway?"

"Sure," Francis answered. The clumsy chat ended when they pulled into the driveway.

Before going inside, Francis grabbed the two newspapers in the flower bed. Anne, never much for keeping up with the news, still received the daily edition for the Arts & Leisure section. Thinking of Summer, Francis strutted alongside his father, up the path through Anne's garden. A corroded brass pineapple knocker was mounted on the front door. The coconut fiber mat said WELCOME.

The afternoon light sliced through the Florida room adjacent to the kitchen. Francis sat down at the table, gazing out onto the dunes that concealed the beach, still wondering how he was going to squeeze in surfing with his dad and going to the movies with Summer.

A giddy Peter returned from the trek up the wooden path that cut through the grassy dunes. From atop the rise behind the house, he had assessed the surf conditions. "Surprise, bud! It's waist-high and glassy. Fun! Let's go!"

Francis liked surfing with his dad, who was sort of a surfing legend, promulgated by his winning the local surf challenge three years in a row, then competing in long-board contests for many years. During that span, he had finished either first or second to the likes of crafty maestro Bobby Chenman or respected board shaper and intrepid surf shop pioneer Bill Frierson. Eventually, Peter joined another divorced, mythical surfing sojourner, Harry Heinke, as one of the few to escape Virginia Beach to another surfing and wahine heaven. Heinke chose Costa Rica, and Peter, of course, stabbed his board in the sand at surfin' USA capital California, adding to the lore. As for Francis, he just liked being in the water with his dad, and he knew how much Peter liked showing off. They hurried to the garage to grab their Frierson boards.

Peter was a master long boarder. Like the Senior Tour of golf, long boarding is often, but not always, the next step for the elder statesmen of the sport who essentially graduate from shredding and slashing on short boards. The rider can catch and ride smaller waves for longer, more luxurious rides on a ten-foot "stick." The best riders can walk around on the board, hanging five or ten in the historical Hawaiian tradition of surf gods. Some can even turn their boards backwards, hang ten on the tail, then spin around and hang ten on the nose. These are the grand old men of the sport, considered legends in local surfing circles.

Thirty years ago, in his teens, after winning several local contests known as Atlantic Coast Surfing Championships, Peter had created a name for himself in the tightly knit adolescent surfing clique for his roving eye for women and glassy offshore break. This reputation continued after he grew older and married Anne. Then, following years of waywardness, he pulled up stakes and escaped to California where he would not have to suffer the stresses of divorcing his wife.

Peter settled in San Diego after brief stops on city staffs in Sausalito and Monterey, landing a job as assistant city manager. His roguish ways continued.

Once, he was out bar hopping in San Diego's Lamplight District with a top developer, when they came across two stunning, tall, and leggy young ladies. The drinks and conversation flowed late into the night. It didn't matter that the developer was married with kids and a pregnant wife. They all ended up at Peter's condo and paired up. It turned out the two ladies were from San Francisco and in San Diego to see a doctor for elective surgery. Of course, this was not part of their lively conversation that night. It would have been quite a mood buster.

After staggering to Peter's one-bedroom flat just a few blocks away and popping champagne, Peter and the developer groped and slobbered over their fine ladies. Peter and one of the lovelies rolled around on his bed, which he called the "snake pit." The developer and his fresh catch of the day were on the couch in the den, watching Peter's porn and getting in the mood, when a ghastly scream came from Peter in the pit. Then several more horrible screams rang out from his lovely lady. Three crashes, five thuds, and four smacks later, Peter came out covered in sweat and a spattering of blood, wearing only his boxers. Let's just say it was the first time there had been more than one snake in the pit! The lovely came staggering out of the room sobbing, nose bloodied. "I tried to tell him! I tried to tell him!"

Peter bolted to the refrigerator and guzzled a beer, swishing and spitting its frothy remains into kitchen sink. The developer jumped off the couch and promptly grabbed his catch in the crotch. "What's this? Oh, my God! No!" He felt it. The horror! His she was a he too!

"Oh, no, I'm gonna be si — " He promptly leaned over the vixen and vomited on her. She screamed in a voice that was strangely a lot deeper than before. The two lovelies ran out the door. Peter and the developer, who weren't the best of friends anyway, swore that the night never happened. They never partied together again, either.

As for the two lovelies, they canceled their elective surgeries, electing instead to keep their respective snakes and move to Amsterdam, where weirdness won't get you punched or puked on.

Peter and Francis went down to the garage, grabbed two boards, and walked through the garden, past the white Adirondack chairs and the hand-woven Hatteras hammock hanging between two sabol palms that bent artfully in opposite directions. Peter led the way over the dunes onto the warm sand. Francis followed, anticipating the shock of the cool, late spring ocean. Once in and paddling out, ducking under the waves, the chill quickly disappeared. Together they steered to where the swells rose. While they sat floating, Francis told his dad about the plans he had made that evening with Summer.

Francis didn't want his dad to be upset that he was going out and cutting short their first night.

Peter's mind drifted from surveying waves until Francis grabbed the first one, a nifty little ride, a perfect, long left. All Peter could do was watch with pride as Francis slashed the face twice in rapid succession, pumped the life out of it as it ebbed, then kicked out and dropped to his belly in one fluid motion. Peter shook his head and smiled.

The late afternoon water grew chilly as they faced the oncoming sea and waited for another choice wave. Off in the distance to the north, a gray warship steamed eastward, having just left the mouth of Chesapeake Bay off Cape Henry. A gargantuan cargo ship followed just a few miles behind, decks piled high with hundreds of multicolored steel containers of American merchandise bound for commercial centers abroad. Peter turned his board toward shore and lay down on his belly. Looking back over his shoulder, he paddled smoothly as the wave picked him up and delivered him into just the right spot for maximum speed and drop. Instinct and the muscle memory of thousands of rides took over as he ripped up the wave. Passing his son, who was heading back out, he felt the familiar rush of pleasure he had longed for all day. Then, as the wave closed into useless white-water mush, he bailed gracefully over the back and dropped to his stomach to paddle out for more. He could see Francis sitting calmly, smiling. A few sets later it was six o'clock, and they rode the last wave to shore, together.

4. "Greenglish"

BOTH OF JOHN CONSTANTINIDES'S PARENTS were Greek. His father, Nicholas, was a postwar baby born in 1948 in Patras, a thriving port city west of Athens, to a large family of hardworking bakers. The bulk of the Constantinides family, including John's great-grandfather, grandmother, uncles, and aunts, had immigrated to the United States decades earlier. Remaining behind to tend the family business interests were Nicholas' father, Alexandros, Nicholas' mother, Sophia, young Nicholas, and his two much older brothers. The family lived and worked on a busy street, operating a popular bakery that sold hearth-baked bread and rolls to locals in the neighborhood. The loaves of bread, *karvelia,* were round and had a crisp crust.

Over time, learning from his now long-assimilated family about their own thriving bakery and other opportunities in the dreamland called The United States of America, Alexandros grew restless. He aspired one day to venture to America and join his family making American-style bread to sell at the unimaginable price of eleven cents per loaf. This, coupled with living in close proximity to a vibrant port and a city of 3 million with numerous international influences, gave Alexandros and his family a glimpse of life outside Greece, whose government was becoming increasingly corrupt and unstable. So, with the encouragement of his Americanized family, he arranged visas and liquidated the bakery and other assets. Finally, in the summer of 1957, Alexandros and his family steamed across the Atlantic to New York, then boarded a train to Baltimore, where the promise of opportunity, a welcoming family, and a lamb roasting on a spit awaited.

Once in Baltimore, Alexandros, Sophia, and the three boys rented a flat downtown near the harbor. Alexandros toiled in the burgeoning bakery while working to gain citizenship for himself and his family. The boys learned English and attended parochial school at the Greek Orthodox Church. After a few years, they went to American public school.

Alexandros worked in the bowels of the plant, and was eventually put in charge. After school, Nicholas would help him, lured by the smell of fermenting dough along with fresh, hot bread coming out of huge ovens. Within a few years, Nicholas knew every oven, dough mixer, conveyor, and dough divider. If a piece of equipment broke, he knew how to fix it fast. Often, he would be called to repair downed ovens in the dead of night so the route salesmen would always have fresh bread the next day. Alexandros grew very proud of his youngest son, who, after he graduated from high school, was soon promoted.

Sadly, sibling rivalry and greed crept into the brotherhood, despite Alexandros' best efforts to treat all three brothers equally. And so, due to his success as a production superintendent, and even though Alexandros had arranged that Nicholas and his brothers would someday operate the family business as partners, Nicholas was considered a threat by his white-collar, older siblings. All the while, the business blossomed. The place had grown from a bakery where folks ordered their fresh bread over a counter, to a wholesale bakery with route sales throughout the Baltimore metro area.

By the late 1970s, Betty Sue Bakery had over a hundred routes providing bread and rolls to restaurants and supermarkets from

Baltimore to Richmond. In 1980, family patriarch Alexandros died, and the three brothers were entrusted with the multimillion-dollar operation. They squabbled about most everything, and as good as he was at producing enormous amounts of bread, Nicholas' financial savvy was lacking. He had invested poorly in the stock market and was over-leveraged, paying 18 percent interest in a depressed real estate market. He had bought a marina in Florida that hemorrhaged $20,000 a month and a shopping center in Fairfax that was only 30 percent leased. Nicholas considered personal bankruptcy, despite his large income from Betty Sue.

Disagreements mounted, and soon the two older brothers wanted Nicholas out. Motivated by what they saw as his financial weakness, they colluded, and attempted to break the trust agreement established as their father's dying wish. After several years of legal wrangling and lawsuits, they bought out all of their unfortunate brother's shares in the bakery for $3.5 million.

After paying off his debts, selling his stocks, and auctioning his real estate interests, a bitter Nicholas had a modest nest egg left. Downtrodden and betrayed, he left Baltimore and, along with his new wife, Mary, moved to sunny Virginia Beach. Like many brilliant Greeks, Nicholas decided to open a restaurant.

He bought a nice four-bedroom colonial in Bay Colony, next to North Beach, with enough left over to purchase a restaurant property from the Papadoupolis family, who had been there for twenty-five years and were ready to retire on the proceeds of the sale. He called the eatery none other than Nick's Steak and Seafood House.

Located on the fringe of the resort area, it was a place that could have existed forty years before. Menu selections were figured to the penny, and nothing was served that did not meet Nicholas' precise 25 percent food-cost standard. The fish was served fried or broiled. The steak was usually boot leather, but the rolls were always good. If a poor server was caught throwing away a pat of margarine, he or she was scolded harshly in "greenglish," a mix of Greek and English.

The plates were hard plastic. The only half-decent thing besides the rolls was the baklava, which was made by Nicholas' wife. After the restaurant had been open for several years and they'd settled into beach living, she finally became pregnant. When she delivered a son, John, Nicholas couldn't have been prouder.

The Constantinides family went to church a half hour away in Norfolk. Nicholas progressed in the church leadership and served on the board. Mary helped with the cooking at various church functions. Son John became an altar boy and joined the Greek youth group called GOYA, the Greek Orthodox Youth Association. He went to most all the Greek festivals and performed with the church's Greek dance troupe in full traditional regalia. He learned to speak Greek fluently and memorized the weekly church service called the Divine Liturgy. By the time John was twelve, he knew every step, every word.

As a nine-year-old, John had started working at Nick's as a bus-boy. When he was thirteen, already almost six feet tall with black curly locks, blue eyes, and the beginnings of a deep voice, John was often mistaken for sixteen or seventeen. Waitresses at Nick's flirted with him, pinching him on the butt or jokingly trying to dance with him in the kitchen, brushing against him as if they were on a dance floor. But John didn't horse around much with them. Dutifully, he stayed busy sweeping the floor or greeting diners as they entered. John was at his best, however, as a hawker. A born natural, he would stand, menu in hand, outside the front door and lure tourists in from the hot, crowded sidewalk with a charming "Hello, how are you this beautiful evening?"

He would add, "Are you looking for a great place to eat?"

Or he'd strike up a conversation with, "Where are you from?"

Then, at the perfect time, he would unfold the menu and go for the kill: "Take a look at our outstanding menu. We have the best chef around." A little lie never hurt. "He's been with us for many years, and we have the best prices on the beach. It's cool inside, and, luckily, it's not that busy right now, so we can get you a nice table near the window. Are there four of you?" Ninety percent of the time, they'd answer yes, which did not go unnoticed by Nicholas.

In Nicholas' mind, John had grown to be everything he had hoped for, and, as Nicholas had done for his father, Alexandros, John would follow in his footsteps. Working in the family business next to his father and serving in the Greek Orthodox Church indicated a comfortable allegiance to a way of life that drew strength from such commitments. Beautifully painted Biblical scenes and carved icons of the great saints, intricately crafted arches, elaborate stained glass, the pungent aroma of aged candle wax, lingering ceremonial incense, the sweet taste of blessed wine, the delicious bread of Christ, the flickering of candles prayed upon by loved ones, and enormous crystalline chandeliers adorned the great hall, overwhelming the senses. Nowhere else in town but the Greek Orthodox Cathedral of Norfolk had all these things, so it was easy to fall in love. It might as well have been the world to young John, as it was for his father and mother.

But as John grew older, things Greek represented a familiarity that, while safe and sure, began to feel restrictive. The ritual of being Greek, and thereby living out a life that seemed predetermined by previous generations, symbolized a "greekification" process that John began to resent. He started to pull away from his family and his culture.

All the while, everyone, Greek and non-Greek, seemed drawn to John's natural charisma and youthful charm, which of course paid dividends in the restaurant trade. But despite all of John's salesmanship working weekends that spring, Nick's had the makings of yet another season a little slower than the last. Cash reserves were shrinking. Additionally, as the school year ended, though Nicholas didn't know it, John wasn't planning to return for another summer.

On a warm, early morning the previous spring, as the sun beamed in the window, thirteen-year-old John sat down for his first-bell class, English Composition. Pale yellow and brown colors washed the room. As the other students shuffled for their seats, Summer Overton walked in and, as always, gracefully slid into one of the last empty chairs in the front row next to him. John's eyes shifted toward her as he leaned back in his chair, ankles crossed.

The teacher, Tyrone Ramsey, had been at First Colony Prep for twenty-five years. His voice had an elegant, international flair that one could only describe as effeminate. The tall, dark African American wore wire-rimmed spectacles, sported a well-groomed goatee, and was known to have had little tutoring get-togethers with his favorite students in the privacy of his home. Over the years, rumors circulated. These rumors were fueled primarily by the tendency to presume that various shenanigans must have occurred from time to time. The mysterious Ramsey evoked fear, disgust, and ridicule from most of his students, especially the boys, yet many were oddly drawn to him by his willingness to allow them the privilege of being in his inner circle.

"Remember where you are today, because that is where you'll sit next year if you don't pass the final," he warned, sounding a lot like a man who had lived in England for a long spell. In his class, everything hinged on the final exam. He continued his rant. "Your exam will consist of one question about which you will write an answer complete with introductory paragraph, thesis statement, well-developed paragraphs supporting your thesis, and a tidy conclusion that wraps the whole thing up in a nice little bow. You will spell and punctuate your answer correctly. You may have a dictionary handy. If you fail this exam, you will fail my class. And don't forget: your reports are due on my desk next class. A late report will result in a grade of "F." Well, boys and girls, this is life with Ramsey. Any questions?"

John took a deep breath and shifted in his seat. Summer glanced at him.

Like many at The Academy, they had been classmates since the

31

first grade. "Can you believe that guy? Man," John whispered looking straight ahead, "we all know the drill. But it's like he gets off on talking to us like we're idiots or something."

Summer just listened and smiled. They both knew that nobody ever failed Ramsey's English class.

After class or on the bus, John would listen, as he had since first grade, to Summer talk about her life, her family, and things thirteen-year-olds talk about. But months before, as cold nor'easters signaled the approaching end of fall, the two had begun to hang out less.

One spring day the next school year, Ramsey quietly passed the word that he was having his traditional mid-semester party at his house. Other teachers were invited as well as students. He envisioned a quaint gathering of youthful intelligentsia at his home, which was stocked with a library, a collection of African and Middle Eastern art, and exotic travel memorabilia. John decided to go.

In the car on the way to Ramsey's, John fidgeted in his seat and tapped his foot to a beat in his head. They passed the impressive beachfront homes that lined Ocean Avenue along the way to the tenured teacher's house.

"So, thees eez English study group?" Nicholas inquired, making conversation, but also curious about his son's schooling. It was important to get good grades. Good grades were everything.

"Sort of, yeah," John replied distantly.

"Whaddya mean, 'Sort of, yeah'?"

John, not wanting his father to know he was headed to a party, answered abruptly with a note of sarcasm, "Some kids are meeting at Mr. Ramsey's house to study in a group to improve their English grade. That makes it an English study group."

"Why can't you do thees in school? Ees Sunday. They can't teach you good enough during the week? I'ma pay all this money for you to have to go to study group."

John knew it was time to be quiet. "How come you hava problem school?" Nicholas didn't want an answer. He was just getting wound up.

"You come home with books for to study. Then the music comes! To study ees quiet in your room. Not noisy. Your mama raise you good, son," adding, "You don't go to tsurts no more. You are head altar boy, for chrissake! How come you don't play for tsurts besketball team no more? What a happen my boy? You good boy."

John had heard this speech ever since he could remember. His dad would always ride him about something, asking questions he didn't want honest answers for, and always ending with "You good boy." Now John was in the midst of changes. So, he thought it best to listen and keep his mouth shut until Nicholas was done lecturing. They pulled into Ramsey's driveway and parked. Then he opened the car door and stepped onto the cool, faux cobblestone driveway.

"Call me when you ready come home," Nicholas said as John closed the car door.

"Sure, Dad," John said as he turned away and walked toward the historic, two-story North Beach Victorian.

A private schoolteacher's pay could not support the expense of the Ramsey home, nestled in a wooded community of predominantly beach cottages, ranch-style houses, and the occasional mansion. Nor could it support the lifestyle of a world traveler. Ramsey had inherited well. People spoke of his wealthy European parents who had died in a plane crash many years ago, leaving him millions.

As John walked up to the door and knocked, he felt exuberant, like he was on the verge of discovering something new and wanted to show off what had been welling up inside the "good boy" who knew the Divine Liturgy by heart.

A smiling Ramsey opened the door. "Good to see you, Sir John," he said formally, reaching out his hand, which John shook awkwardly. "Glad you could make it. Please come in."

John walked into a dimly lit foyer where some of his classmates huddled together. Some older kids he had seen around school but did not know were there, as well as a few others he didn't recognize. Classical music, loud talk, laughter, and clove cigarette smoke wafted throughout the house. The aroma, though distinctly different, reminded him a little of the holy incense at church.

Ramsey motioned across the room to beyond the open living room doorway. "We've got ginger-ale punch. There's plenty to eat in the kitchen. Look, the spinach dip is over there. Oh, you know Stuart. Stuart, look who's here, John Constantinides."

Stuart rode the bus and surfed with John and Francis. He was also one of the "brains" in school, a title reserved for those borderline geniuses destined for future scholarships to schools like Amherst, Harvard, Princeton, or nearby William and Mary. Attending The Academy on a financial aid scholarship awarded when he was tested and scored in the upper one-tenth percentile, he never got below an "A." Wearing a loose, unbuttoned aloha party shirt over a white T-shirt and jeans pulled up too high, he looked like the classic computer geek on vacation. The truth was, he came from the other side of the tracks and an unenviable life.

"Hi, John. How's it goin'?" Stuart inquired with noticeable curiosity. Seeing John in a social setting was much different.

"Oh, fine, I guess. But I forgot to bring some food over like everyone else who's trying to improve their grades around here." Then he looked to Ramsey, who stood there, hands on hips, feigning offense at John's rude remark. John had made a grand entrance and felt a rush of fearlessness. Stuart, who grinned widely and held back a laugh, playfully put an elbow in John's ribs.

Ramsey was unflustered. "Mr. Constantinides"—the "Sir" had vanished—"you may help yourself to the bribery offerings in the kitchen." He pointed a bony finger across the room toward the open doorway, then turned and started a dialog with someone nearby.

For an instant, the babble of many overlapping conversations became distinct to John. He differentiated each within earshot: the three fifteen-year-old girls talking about their lousy parents; the two senior boys carrying on about their last rehearsal for the school play; even four of his classmates' ruthless whispering about Ramsey's sexual inclinations. Stuart interrupted John's acute moment.

"I can't believe what you just did! You blew him away. How– I mean, what…? Wow!" Stuart was nearly speechless.

John wasn't interested in talking about it. He was still caught in his moment of fearlessness and clarity. *Is this what it feels like to be a grownup?* he thought. It seemed a whole new world was just beginning to open up to him. "Let's go into the kitchen and check out the eats."

They were a curious match, John and Stuart, but from that moment, they became more than kids who sometimes surfed the same beach; they became pals and hung together that summer, often meeting at the beach or hanging out on the sidewalk outside the arcade.

Later that evening, back in the living room, John was chatting it up with two of his classmates when Ramsey interrupted. "John, I want to have a word with you. Would you excuse us?" he asked firmly, yet politely.

John left his new friends and followed Ramsey to the study. Hundreds of old books and papers stuffed into built-in wooden bookcases and stacked on antique tables filled the dimly lit room. "What possessed you to speak to me that way earlier tonight?" Ramsey started. "I won't have that in my class and certainly not in my house."

"I'm sorry, Mr. Ramsey. I was only kidding," John said, retreating.

The teacher took the offensive. "I will not tolerate being accused of giving preferential treatment." As he got more worked up, Ramsey's voice rose to a high pitch that John found amusing.

"What do you want me to do?" John asked. "I said I was sorry."

Ramsey paused for a moment, then smiled, putting his hand lightly on John's shoulder. "Let's stop this nonsense. You have taken the time to come to my home. Frankly, I am delighted you decided to do so. Nonetheless, I believe you are here for a reason, perhaps unknown to you. I have high hopes for you, Sir John. Let me help you unleash your writing abilities by tutoring you after school for a while. I could help you over the summer, and you'll be ahead of the kids next year. Once a week for one hour would be plenty; how about it?"

John hesitated, not prepared for the offer. For the kid who could persuade tourists with dozens of dining options to choose Nick's, his English composition skills needed some work. But what about the gay rumors? Queasy at the unsavory thoughts, John managed a smile and nodded. As for rumors, he didn't care much what others thought. Like most kids at The Academy, he needed the grades.

≋

Life at the Constantinides home often consisted of Nicholas sitting in the leather easy chair watching news channels, while his wife created intoxicating aromas in the kitchen and waited on him hand and foot. John stayed in his room with the door closed most of the time; an icon of Saint John the Baptist looked down from above the doorway. His window overlooked the front yard, where he could see his father pull up after work or watch the neighbors move about.

Since he'd been a small child, John had been fascinated with World War II. Model Sherman and Panzer tanks decorated his bookcase among the many books, most on Greece, which were popular birthday and Christmas presents. Flying Tigers, German spitfires, and other planes of the era hung from the ceiling. A fleet of gray warships sat on his dresser, lined up in perfect order. The stark white walls were covered with pictures of Greek ruins and posters of the war movies: *Patton*, *Bridge Over the River Kwai*, *Sniper*, and *Saving Private Ryan*. Arnold Schwartzenegger from the movie *Predator* loomed over John's bed.

By the end of spring semester, John's grades improved, and a mentoring relationship with Ramsey had developed. Whatever awkwardness there had been subsided.

An unseasonably warm Friday evening, Ramsey dropped John off at home, which had become the routine, much later than usual. The problem was that the busy dinner rush had already started at Nick's, and John was scheduled to work. Nicholas waited angrily at the front door, arms crossed. As John walked up the steps, the interrogation began.

"Ees a Friday night, ees eighty degrees, ees 7:15, and you come home. I wait for you when I should be in restaurant. But I want to see when you come. What are you doing? You know the restaurant ees busy, and I wait here for to tek you to work. Who ees thees teesher kep you late? I don like eet, son. Hurry and a change you close." He paused and took a breath. "I don' know what you think about these days," he concluded.

"Not going anymore," said John abruptly.

"Excuse me?"

"I quit the restaurant." This was the boldest John had ever been with his father.

Nicholas delayed for a moment, stunned by his son's brazenness. He gathered himself and recommenced his diatribe. "Ever since you grow up, you been acta funny ... not like my son. You mother and I raise you up to be good, honest boy, to respect. Lately, you by youself. I don't know what you think about. Now, you go tutor and come home later and later—mees work. I meet thees English teesher last year. He seem a leetle strange to me."

John now realized that his newfound A's didn't matter to his father. It didn't even matter if he worked at the restaurant. It was only important that he be who his father thought he should be. But he wasn't any of that at all. And now, it seemed so simple; he just wouldn't put up with it anymore. *From now on,* he thought, *I'm in charge.*

At a loss, Nicholas turned away, fuming, and walked to the car. The sky was clear and still. John sat on the front steps. He could hear the distant clanking sounds of his mother washing dishes in the kitchen, her silhouette behind the drawn shade. Nicholas drove to the restaurant by himself.

The next day, John lay on his bed. He gazed up at warplanes and looked forward to hooking up with Stuart to check out the shops that lined Beach Boulevard. There was a head shop that always stayed packed, a body-piercing and tattoo parlor that usually had people waiting, a couple of go-go bars, some seedy restaurants and clubs, and a pawnshop that sold just about anything to anybody. He and Stuart met outside Joker's, the head shop.

"What's up, bro?" Stuart said with his best rapper imitation.

"Just hangin'," John replied, getting into the act.

"Whew!" Stuart cried out, holding his fist out for John to punch. They tapped knuckles, walked by Joker's, and went into Half Moon.

They liked the weird techno background music and photos of half-naked, tattooed women on the walls. For two fourteen-year-olds, it was fun to check out the magazines, especially the grotesque pictures of people with tattoos and piercings covering their bodies. The boys laughed and made noises of shock and amazement in the waiting room of the pristine parlor, irritating the manager who, after about five minutes, emerged from the back. He wore a wife-beater tank top, had a dozen or so piercings in his ears, one loop in each eyebrow, a tongue bolt, and tattoos visible on both arms, across his shoulders, and up his neck.

"Hey, fellas, you want somethin'?" he asked gruffly.

The boys hurriedly slapped the magazine down, got up from the steel chairs, and moved toward the door. Stuart thought about what it would be like to have his tongue pierced or get a tattoo on his forearm. John thought the manager looked funny, cartoonish.

"Let's go, Stu," John said, laughing nervously. They turned away and hustled out the door in the direction of Bob's Pawn to check out guns and knives. The adventure ended with an ice-cream cone and a slice of pizza.

Later that day, Nicholas came home for a rare break from the restaurant, arriving to the thumping of music upstairs and the smell of last night's dinner. He sat in the den with the newspaper, passing over the headlines on global warming and turning to the back of the business section to see the weather page. He shook his head grimly at the revised forecast of wind and rain for at least three days. Nick's needed the revenue, and a three-day storm would kill business.

The restaurant was situated on the outskirts of the hotel-packed, family-oriented resort area that transformed into a traffic jam most of the summer. The sidewalks teemed with every type of character imaginable, from mamas with babies in tow to hip-hop-gangsta wannabes. City planners dealt with all the social ills, especially late at night, that intruded on a carefully crafted image of family-friendly hospitality. Smart locals learned to avoid the nightly traffic jam and rowdy party vibe, while tourists realized the best way to get around, day or night, was on foot.

Driving had become next to impossible as tourism exploded in the packed hotel and retail hub. Planners encouraged walking or riding the fifty-cent public trolley, which stopped seven blocks south of Nick's and looped back into the heart of the resort, also called "The Strip." Nicholas complained about the unfairness of the trolley route and how it not only hurt his business but also favored his competitors. The truth of the matter was Nicholas' operation was a dying breed, now giving way to trendier restaurants with new-American cuisine. It looked like another bad year for Nick's.

As he sat on the floral couch in the den and drank his coffee, Nicholas could hear John crank up his stereo. His head pounded with each beat. He gritted his teeth reflexively. The music had no words, just a steady pulse and synthesized rhythm. It was the music John had heard at the body-piercing studio.

The den smelled of mothballs combined with years of Greek cooking. Its brown paneled walls were sparsely decorated with a hodgepodge of collectible plates, and the worn, tan carpet needed cleaning. The coffee table boasted a brass Trojan horse and a plastic model of the Acropolis atop a dusty, eight-by-ten wooden icon of Jesus carrying His cross. Pursing his lips, Nicholas sighed and shook his head, then slowly, deliberately, put his coffee down on the table. Neatly setting his paper aside, he started toward the stairs.

Nicholas slowly trudged up the narrow stairs until he stood outside John's room. Since John had quit his restaurant and altar boy duties, Nicholas had concocted the story that John had to study harder for school; that he was concentrating on getting the best grades he could in order to go to a good college. This was the story he told when asked questions like, "What's John doing these days?" or "I don't see Yannie at tsurts. Is he oikay?" As he recited the tale over and over, Nicholas almost started to believe it himself, that is, until the pounding music coming from John's room reminded him otherwise. It seemed to him that the volume grew louder by the day, and the family pictures were going to fall off the walls from the beat of the subwoofer. He reached for the doorknob and turned it both ways. He was locked out. Nicholas paused, remembering the day John was born and how he sped from the restaurant to pass out cigars and hold "leetle Yannie." Then, putting his hands on either side of the doorjamb, he bent his head and wept. His shoulders heaved with the force of his sobs, as tears poured down his rough face. The noise from John's room drowned out his father's crying.

5. A Summer Date

Summer thought about what she would wear on her date with Francis and friends. It was a warm night, and an arch of sweat traced her upper lip. She slipped on a yellow sundress. Its spaghetti straps showed off her growing femininity and outlined her tanned shoulders and back. She turned from side to side and smiled at her reflection in the full-length mirror on her closet door. *Not too revealing,* she thought. Her dancing blue eyes were framed by silky blond hair that fell loosely over her shoulders. She thought of Francis and how cute he was. She imagined his soft skin next to hers. He exuded a childlike vulnerability and quiet sensitivity that attracted her.

"Summer, it's time to go," her mother, Rose, called.

The Overtons were a close family in which conversation flowed freely, and dysfunction was invisible. They attended a newly formed, charismatic church in the suburbs, led by Pastor Mark Magiani. Her father, Bill, conducted a Wednesday night Bible study group at their North Beach house. The study group often turned into a cocktail party, with Rose laying out food for everyone. Summer would stay up and, at times, participate in the pseudo-spiritual discourse, then it was off to bed as Bibles closed, corks popped, and adult time commenced with celebration of Jesus' first miracle. But tonight was

41

different. Summer felt a little more grown-up at the prospect of going out with her parents.

After the sitter arrived to watch Summer's younger brother, Steve, the plan was to pick up Francis and meet Summer's friends at Mike's Pizza. Then her parents would go out for dinner somewhere fancy, and afterward pick the kids up from the nearby movie theater.

Bill, Rose, and Summer arrived at Francis' and honked. Francis bounded out the door, wearing his favorite white Roccawear shirt, tan baggies, and Hawaiian-style sandals. Waving to his parents, he climbed into the back of the huge Suburban with Summer. It was Francis' first real date.

With Francis out for the night, Peter prepared for his own night on the town. He put on his Issey Miyake cologne and aqua-blue Perry Ellis pullover and cruised over to the nearest watering hole. He bellied up to the locals' bar at the North Beach Grill, a loud place where the drinks were expensive and the women were semi-sophisticated. Peter surveyed the busy drinkery, looking for someone he knew or the happenstance of a demure woman registering on his finely tuned radar screen. Three Belvedere vodka martinis later, he managed to meet and hold court with two North Beach foxes in their mid-thirties. He couldn't have cared less about them, but they looked good just the same. As the night wore on, old chums trickled in, making Peter quite the popular native son come home.

The evening became a reunion of sorts, with old surf and party pals coming over to slap him on the back and catch up on the local gossip—mainly, who had divorced whom and which developers were fighting over the last remaining scraps of decent oceanfront land. In the midst of draining his fourth monster martini, Peter thought about Francis growing up without him. Then the night became a blur. Thoroughly anesthetized, finally, the surfer legend slithered out the door, got in his ex-wife's car, and headed to what once was his home and a family that had belonged to him a decade ago. Somehow pulling into the narrow driveway without destroying the mailbox, Peter staggered up the path to the front door.

After the tenth knock, Anne appeared at the door with a familiar scowl. "Well, I see some things don't change. You can't blame me anymore for being a lush, can you, mister bachelor in California for how many years now?"

"Lemme alone. I need water and aspirin," Peter slurred. Disgusting olive and vodka breath had replaced the fine aroma of his top-shelf cologne.

"Whew, you stink. Go over to the couch." Anne left for the kitchen to grant his highness' request.

Peter proceeded to plop down and watch TV. While Anne rummaged for aspirin in the kitchen, Francis bounded through the front door and into the den where Peter snored and Letterman blared in the background. Anne hugged Francis tightly. Peter struggled to compose himself. Awkwardly, he sat up on the couch. For an instant, Francis saw a family.

"Francis, uh … how was the movie?" Peter asked.

"Good."

"It's almost midnight. What did you do after the movie?" Anne was only curious, trusting her son, as well as the very Christian Overtons.

"We hung out at Summer's and talked for a while. The Overtons are really nice."

"Did you have a good time with the kids?" Anne asked."

"Yeah, only I didn't talk much with them because Summer and I talked a lot, except during the movie, of course."

"What did you guys talk about?" Peter fought his spinning head and thick tongue, not wanting his son to notice his drunkenness.

Francis laughed, "'Daaaad, stop being so nosy."

They all laughed together. Then Francis went to bed.

Late that night, a storm blew in. At first light the next morning, Francis turned over and gazed out his second-floor window. He thought of Summer while watching the turbulent waves buffet the shoreline. He noticed a few rideable sets. Shaking his head at the foolishness of his thoughts, he headed for the stairs. Francis knew the idea of surfing on the washing machine-like sea was crazy, but today he was drawn to the rush.

Despite his alertness, the house felt lifeless. Goose bumps rolled up his spine as he tiptoed down the stairs toward the garage to choose his board. The wind howled. Next to the boards, Francis' array of wetsuits hung in a line. He picked the spring suit his mom had given him for his birthday last year and slipped it over his chubby torso. His breath quickened when he opened the door to the garden, the beach, and the raging surf beyond. His muscles tightened.

Once on the beach, he felt the relentless whipping of the gale. As he walked on the wet, hard sand, the heavy chop and windswept swells seemed to challenge him. Whitecaps danced and beckoned mockingly. *C'mon and try us,* they seemed to say. Francis stood in the foamy sand, rain pelting his face. For an instant, good sense told him to turn back. Then he ran to the break and dove onto his board, paddling straight into the pounding surf.

The waves came from all directions, rising from everywhere and nowhere. Each seemed determined to beat him. Then a wave broadsided him and knocked him off his board. He went under. If not for the leash secured around his ankle and attached to the board, Francis probably would have drowned right there, but he pulled himself up to the surface and managed to slide back onto the board, which had quickly become a life raft. He didn't notice that the long-shore currents had pushed him northward up the beach, way beyond the house. Holding on with his legs and arms, he gained control, and the raft became his surfboard again. He waited for his moment.

Just one ride, he thought, with a strange calm amidst the tempest. After what seemed like only a few seconds, a glassy peak rose above the others. Francis lay flat on his board, then paddled into position to catch the wave. It was twelve feet at the face, the type of wave that could pound a grown man into the hard sand, killing him beneath tons of suffocating force. Francis pivoted as the wave drew him in. Then it was quiet. The breaker loomed overhead. With all his might, he kicked and paddled to stay ahead of the crest beneath the windblown, snarling lip. In one fluid motion, he was up and on his feet, hands holding the board on either side as he crouched. Then he let go of the board and stretched his arms out to gain his balance. Francis rose above the dark waters. He maneuvered, maneuvered again, balanced, balanced again, took one slash up the face, then dropped into a tiny barrel that spat him out and away from the imminent crash as the wave gave way to shallowness. Francis glided to center, surviving the thunderous fall of the breaker as it frothed and fumed behind him. Panting, he coasted to shore on his belly and began the ten-block walk home.

He arrived unnoticed, walked into the garage, carefully hung up his wetsuit, placed his board on the rack, then tiptoed back upstairs to his bedroom. Gazing out the window, beyond the dune, he saw where he had been. It was time to wake up.

Just down the hall, dehydration had Peter in its grip, for he had forgotten to take aspirin and drink the water Anne had given him the night before. His breath was foul, and his head pounded. The storm raged outside. He got up to use the bathroom. After guzzling water from the tap, he crawled back into bed and pulled the sheets up tightly. He slept for two more hours.

The gusts awakened Anne, but she had fallen back to sleep, only to open her eyes again moments later to contemplate what wasn't. Squeezing the pillow tightly between her legs, she imagined a man's arms around her, his breath against her neck. Then another gust shook the house, and she sat up on the edge of her bed, gazing at herself in the mirror that hung on the closet door. Her body was toned and slender from twenty years of working out. Her chest jutted out from the implants she'd added two years after the divorce. Men paid attention to her, but it seemed to Anne that they were always the wrong men.

She slowly shuffled to the adjacent master bath and attended to her morning routine. She dressed in jeans and a sweatshirt and went out for the paper. The door flew open from the force of the wind. Her garden was in shambles. Branches lay all over the yard. She grabbed the paper and started some coffee. She gazed at the front page. The headlines read:

SYRIAN AND IRANIAN CLERICS CALL FOR
JIHAD ON AL-JAZEERA NETWORK

Beneath the header, Anne read:

INSURGENTS KILL 25 AMERICANS IN BLOODBATH

Anne looked out the window as the storm shook her beachfront home. Francis came down the stairs.

"Francis, you're up early for a Saturday. Did you sleep okay?"

"The storm woke me up, and I just started thinking about stuff."

Francis sat at the kitchen table. He could see the article.

"Some kids are saying the Pakistani kids at school are terrorists. But they're just kids."

Anne half listened. She put the paper down and looked in the refrigerator. "That's a shame, honey. But I'm glad you see that," she answered distractedly, as she held the refrigerator door open.

Francis gazed out of the bay window that provided a view of the hilly dunes. The steady rumble of storm-stirred surf reminded him of his adventure that morning.

"Hey, Mom, what's for breakfast?"

"Pancakes, your favorite," Anne answered as she pulled out eggs and milk. Francis loved to watch his mother make pancakes, his anticipation building as she beat the batter smooth. Then she would pour the heavenly mixture onto the flat skillet. The bouquet of the browning cakes overcame the boy, as the aroma of a fine champagne would a wine connoisseur. Finally, when he was about to burst with excitement, the towering plate would appear before him, awash in Log Cabin and oozing warm butter between the layers. By now, ready to leap out of his chair, his eyes would relish the sight for only the briefest moment before his fork would commence destruction of the perfect picture, and Anne's work of art would disappear into his stomach.

The gray morning passed slowly. Peter awoke again and made his way to the kitchen. The three were like a family again. Peter nursed his familiar hangover with his cure-all, tomato juice and a shot of vodka, which he secretly added from the cupboard. He chatted with Anne at the kitchen table about the goings-on in San Diego, while Francis watched TV, thinking about Summer and surfing storms. Anne listened patiently to Peter's recounting of the past ten years. What she noticed was that San Diego was not so different from Virginia Beach. They had essentially the same surf, same navy, same bars, same politicians, and most of all, the same Peter. She could see that he really hadn't left Virginia Beach at all, but rather, had chosen a carbon-copy place and a carbon-copy life. The only difference was the absence of family and the time since the day he'd left.

Back at the Overtons' household, life seemed less painful. Up early due to the racket from the storm, Bill and Rose sat together at the breakfast table, planning a weekend trip to the hills of Virginia to tour vineyards and make love in quaint bed and breakfasts.

"Let's start at the Inn at Little Washington," Bill suggested. "Prince Michel and Barboursville wineries are nearby, and the inn is rated five stars by Mobil."

"I've always wanted to go there, but isn't it rather expensive?" She raised an eyebrow at him.

Bill had inherited the Overton family fortune eight years ago, but Rose handled the family finances.

He grinned and patted her hand. "Yes, but we can fit it into our budget."

"Okay, okay," she giggled. "I'll let my female side get the better of my frugal side!" Rose still worked in an antique and fine art gallery, even though she didn't have to. She liked her own money and didn't mind spending Bill's.

Summer, yawning, joined them in the kitchen. She was wearing a pair of Rose's flip-flops.

"Bill, do you remember that quaint bed and breakfast we drove by in Middleburg after the Gold Cup last year? I think it was called the Red Fox Inn. Middleburg's such a picturesque town."

The Gold Cup was a steeplechase horse race they went to each fall with a group of close friends. It was basically a tailgate party where everyone shared food, drank too much, and ignored the races.

"Yeah, honey, that sounds good. I know a few vineyards out that way, too," Bill answered.

Summer checked the refrigerator. "Good morning," her parents said, almost in unison, without taking their eyes off the travel brochures spread about the breakfast table.

The wind howled, and rain fell in diagonal sheets. Summer moved aside some of the unfolded brochures and maps to make room for her cereal and orange juice and sat down at the end of the table. Her plans for the day, a beach party with her church youth group, were scrapped by the weather, so she thought of indoor things to do.

Her mouth was soon crammed with Froot Loops. She liked to pack in as many as she could and let the cold milk intermingle with the crunchy sweetness until the cereal became soft and mushy. "Hey, Mom," she said with a mouthful, "I need a bathing suit and some other stuff for summer. Can we go to the mall?"

Rose replied, happy at the prospect of a girls' day out, "Sure, and let's get some lunch at the new sushi bar. Will you be ready in half an hour?"

"No problem." She scooped another spoonful. Switching gears, she turned to Francis. "So, Dad, didn't you think Francis was soooo nice? I think he's cute. We talked about school and stuff. He's really interested in what's going on. He might be class president someday. I mean, he didn't really talk about that, but I think so. And he surfs with his dad when he comes to visit, or sometimes he gets up real early and goes by himself. Only, it's a secret. You promise not to tell?"

"Of course, honey," Rose replied instead, as Bill pondered the inn's wine list.

"Did I tell you guys Francis' dad was visiting from California?" Then, back to Francis, "Anyway, he's soooo nice."

Excitedly, Summer shoveled in more Froot Loops, gulped down the last of her orange juice, then ran upstairs to get ready.

"I wonder when Francis' voice is gonna change?" Bill quipped in a hushed tone, winking at Rose. The two continued their planning as rain rapped the house.

Upstairs, Summer prepared for the outing with her mother. She had grown up going to her parents' church, where they preached vigilance against the incursions of Satan. So, when she was finished dressing, she knelt beside her bed, gazed upward, and said her prayers to God and Jesus. Summer's prayers included everyone: parents, classmates, poor kids, sick people, even animals. She was, in a sense, a new breed of pure American girl. Summer talked to God and Jesus every morning before leaving her room for the day. This was what she was taught at the New Hope Evangelical Church.

6. Storm Clouds

~~~~~~

Stuart called John's house late in the morning, after Nicholas had left for work. Once, several months before, Nicholas had caught Stuart and John in the basement looking at *Penthouse* and *Hustler* magazines they had taken from Stuart's stepdad. Nicholas had confiscated the porn and chewed out the boys, so Stuart avoided all interaction with him and knew to call John after ten, when Nicholas always was gone. John, who was wearing baggy camouflage shorts and no shirt, picked up the phone in his dad's office on the first ring.

"Hello."

"Yo, bro," Stuart started, "let's hit The Strip—check out Bob's Pawn."

"It's raining like crazy," John complained.

"So what? Didn't stop Rambo, did it?"

"Okay, GI Joe, when do you want to hook up?"

"Two."

"See ya there—over and out."

The notion of hanging out on The Strip in the rain with Stuart really didn't interest John that much, but his lack of enthusiasm wasn't all Stuart's fault; rather, it was the prospect of another dull summer. From early June until the start of school in late August, the waves would likely be flat, the sun blazing, and the days long, especially since he was now officially unemployed. The only thing that offered the prospect of excitement was the .38 he knew was locked in Nicholas' desk drawer. But today would be just another trip to The Strip with Stuart.

≋

After a slow, rainy start to the summer and even without the services of ace hawker "Yannie," business at Nick's started booming. Nicholas had come up with a brilliant idea. He would run full-page ads in a widely circulated weekly tourist magazine, giving away free fried flounder or choice beef kabobs with purchase of any entrée from 4:30 to 6:30 every day. When the sun finally emerged midsummer, and tens of thousands of full-color ads hit the streets with the header nicholas gives it away, lines of hungry tourists wrapped around the restaurant. Coupon clippers rejoiced — it was the best deal in town, an offer the hungry masses couldn't refuse.

Before this ad ran, Nick's was usually empty, and an empty restaurant is bad for business. *Must be the food,* passersby had thought as they peeked in. Now, the passé eatery was packed, and the lines outside drew the attention of pedestrians, even after the special ended. The throngs slowly ambled, as if hypnotized, to the rear of the queue and waited. Folks lined up every evening for Nicholas' food — the very same food that he'd served for years — paying tourist-trap prices all night long until a tired Nicholas locked the door at 11 p.m.

One evening after everyone had gone home, Nicholas sat in his usual corner booth and tallied receipts over a milky glass of ouzo on the rocks. Sales had quadrupled. Listening to the hum of twenty compressors and a neon open sign, Nicholas chuckled. For the first time since the summer he'd opened the restaurant, he felt optimistic. *Nick's will make it after all,* he thought. He drained the glass and got up. On his way across the dining room, he bumped into a table with four captain's chairs stacked on it. A chair fell to the floor as he stumbled toward the cocktails sign. Once behind the bar, he dipped the silver scoop into the ice and added a few cubes, then turned and pulled a quarter-full bottle of Metaxa from the shelf, emptying it into his tall glass. The liquid turned milky. He took a swig. Then, surveying the empty restaurant, he slammed his meaty hand down on the bar. His fleeting chuckle became a sob. At home, behind a locked bedroom door, was a boy he no longer knew. Where had John gone?

On a muggy morning a few days later, as Nicholas drank his coffee at the breakfast table and read the paper, he saw the headline: Plans for 800-Room Timeshare and Hotel Resort Complex at Oceanfront.

Anxiously reading the article, Nicholas realized that the area chosen for this enormous, unprecedented project was very near his restaurant. He learned that developers and city planners had gotten together and decided it was time to construct a "first-class," forty-story skyscraper that would displace supposedly blighted properties and be a beacon for further progress and development. The article went on to say that the plans for the multifaceted, multibillion-dollar venture would go before the city council for a vote in two months. If approved, and after passing a few other hurdles, the developers would break ground in eighteen months. Reading on, Nicholas realized that the proposed complex was more than near his restaurant—the planned time-share/hotel and its public parking garage was right on top of it!

Nicholas slammed down the paper, dug into the kitchen drawer, and pulled out the phone directory. Rifling the pages, he tore out the government listings, stopping at "Mayor's Office." He was routed to the mayor's secretary, who, surprisingly, put his call straight through. The mayor listened graciously and finally suggested that Nicholas contact his councilman, attend planning sessions, and "be a part of the process." Upset and fearful, Nicholas hung up the phone. He gulped down his coffee and dutifully went to work at his restaurant, leaving a wayward son and long-suffering wife at home.

On this same morning at the Hickses', Stuart stirred about the house, awakened by the usual racket of his stepfather Carl's arrival from the graveyard shift at 7-Eleven. He passed by his fun-loving half sister's room, where she and this month's boyfriend slept. Down the hall, the door to Stuart's stepdad's room was wide open, revealing piles of clothes, beer cans, and fast-food wrappers. Carl lounged in the beat-up La-Z-Boy in the middle of the den, devouring a breakfast burrito and Big Gulp. He was certainly a true 7-Eleven company man, a product of the product, aptly glued to a rerun of "Jerry Springer." Saying nothing to the zombie in the den, Stuart walked by without offering the slightest acknowledgment. He went to his room and closed the door behind him.

Stuart was one of two students who attended First Colony Prep on a full scholarship for gifted but underprivileged kids. Believing her boy had superior intelligence, Stuart's mother, Samantha, had him tested at age five. It was determined that he really was exceptional and might be eligible for financial assistance at a private school. Stuart was soon admitted to one in Norfolk, but the school administrators felt that, despite getting good grades, he lacked the maturity to advance to the second grade. Rather than have him repeat at the same school, they recommended The Academy. So, Stuart's mom enrolled him at age six.

Back when Stuart was four, Samantha, after two and a half turbulent years of marriage to the abusive Carl, had left the family for Florida with a used car salesman. Six months later, when he dumped her, she returned home. Carl did not care much for her coming back, but he needed someone to keep house. Eight months later, Samantha was diagnosed with pancreatic cancer. In less than a year she was dead.

Amber balanced a cell phone and an iron with ease. Born out of wedlock to a seventeen-year-old Samantha, she had years of practice, living through her mother's string of husbands, an ugly divorce, and then Carl. After Samantha took sick, Amber again took up the job of mothering and keeping house while stepdad went to go-go bars, watched TV, or complained about the clientele at the 7-Eleven where he toiled as manager. His favorite pastime was drinking Milwaukee's Best in front of the TV and watching late-night porn. Amber, a continuously ringing cell in hand, worshipped at the altar of have a good time. Oftentimes, the altar was her mattress.

When, as a young child, Stuart first heard the strange sounds coming from his sister's bedroom, he thought Amber might be sick. He pressed his ear to her door and listened. The barking noises sounded familiar, not because dogs bark, but because the same yelps came from porn stars he had seen on Carl's TV in the den. Nauseated, he slid down the door and sat on the carpet. As the headboard steadily rapped the wall, sweat beaded on Stuart's brow and the narrow hallway began to spin. He ran to the toilet to throw up. When he exited the bathroom, a tall, shirtless man about the same age as Carl rammed into him, grunted, and closed the door. Some introduction to the birds and the bees.

Despite her promiscuous ways, Amber fulfilled many motherly duties well: she did the laundry, shopped with Stuart for clothes, made sure food was in the refrigerator, and occasionally cleaned the house, or at least yelled at Stuart and Pops to get off their butts and clean their messes. She even brought home a little money waitressing so she and Stuart could go to a movie or play a game of putt-putt. One Christmas, Amber got Stuart a surfboard, a really nice one shaped by a local board guru. It was the best present Stuart had ever received. When he saw it, he knew right away it was a "Frierson."

Sequestered in his room, Stuart had time to kill before another rendezvous with John, so he surfed the net, dialed the radio to his favorite DJ, and cranked up some tunes. After a while, the music succeeded in overshadowing the hell of another day. Outside the tiny house, the wind blew the rain sideways, which, along with the music, drowned out the noises coming from his sister's room.

7. It's a Beach Thing

PETER LAY DOWN ON THE COUCH to nurse his hangover and turned on CNN. He thought about flying back to San Diego in a few days and of the moves he would make in the stock market. After a while, Francis appeared. Peter, half dozing, smiled.

Francis began, "Hey Dad, wanna catch a movie or go to the jetty and check out some waves?"

Peter didn't feel like getting up, much less going out. "I'm not really up to it, kiddo. Maybe tonight we could—"

The phone rang a foot away. He jumped. "Hello," he said painfully.

"Is Francis there?" a deep voice asked.

"Sure, hold on. Francis, it's for you." He handed Francis the cordless.

The deep voice was familiar to Francis. "Hey, man, how's it goin'?"

It was John.

"Uh...okay." Surprised, he summoned up his surfing lingo and added, "Just checkin' out the breeze. Pretty rad, huh?" Francis walked down the hall so he could hear John over the noise of the television.

"Hey, Stuart and I are going to ride our bikes down to The Boulevard and check out some stuff we saw the other day." Knowing Francis, John added, "And Bob's Pawn has some new boards. Wanna come?"

John, Stuart, and Francis had attended school and ridden the same bus together since the first grade. The kids' camaraderie was based on their proximity to one another, rather than on any personal traits they shared, aside, of course, from an affinity for surfing. In surf cultures everywhere, that love draws many together who might one day grow up to be doctors, teachers, fitness instructors, artists, or even expatriates. Bank accounts and mansions aside, surfing is and always will be the great equalizer.

Francis, knocked off balance by the invitation, regained his composure. "I don't know if the folks will let me … with the storm and all." He paused a moment. "I'll ask, but Dad's in town, and he might have stuff planned for later."

John implored, "Don't frail on me, dude. What's a little wind and rain?"

"I'll call you back in a few," Francis said.

Francis went into the den where Peter channel surfed. Seeing his son, Peter muted the TV.

"Hey, Dad," Francis began, "is it okay if I cruise down to The Strip and check out boards and maybe some wetsuits with a couple of friends from school? I know it's raining, but I'll put on my poncho … won't be gone long. We could do something later, Dad."

"Sure. I'll tell your mother. Go on, have fun." Peter could rest his head awhile longer and sank gratefully into the pillows.

Francis called John back, and they agreed to meet at Bob's Pawn. He ran to the garage, threw on his poncho, and started pedaling south.

With the northeast wind blowing from behind, Francis could almost coast from his house southward through North Beach. Soon he neared the resort strip, passed by Nick's Restaurant, then the lineup of souvenir shops, T-shirt shops, and pancake places. On the beach side of The Strip, hotels arose from what once was rolling berm, live oaks, and swaying dune grasses. From as far back as the 1920s, savvy developers had built romantic getaway hotels, restaurants, stores, and parking lots smack on top of what had been pristine sands. For good measure they'd added a wooden boardwalk. Now, those charming old seaside inn retreats were gone, replaced by dozens of new hotels and high-rise, 300-room resort properties with eateries serving up $30 fish dinners with trendy sauces from some cooking channel. The old wooden boardwalk had long since been replaced by an elevated seawall and wider concrete boardwalk. The promenade included a six-foot-wide bike path where collisions routinely occurred between eastbound pedestrians gazing bleary-eyed for the first time at the ocean, and tipsy, super-fit locals on beach-cruiser bicycles pedaling north and south from one watering hole to the next. These tangled crashes happened almost as often as red time was sold in the towering timeshare resorts that loomed above the flat, expansive beach.

To keep rising seas back, and in the absence of replenishing dunes, the Army Corps of Engineers periodically pumped black sand onto the beach from offshore in a cleverly named use of federal money called Operation Big Beach. The black silt, loaded with sea life, was then left to dry and bleach in the sun so millions could sprawl and tan their butts each summer. On this stormy day, however, the few tourists there were huddled inside their hotel rooms, leaving the beaches, boardwalk, streets, and sidewalks almost vacant.

Francis turned the corner of Beach Boulevard. Two beach-cruiser bikes perched unchained on the bike rack, but John and Stuart were not inside the pawnshop. Instead, they sat in the window of Half Moon Piercing & Tattoo. Spotting them, Francis went inside.

"Hey, bud, check this one out," chirped Stuart. Francis hesitantly walked over and stood behind them. Stuart and John were flipping through magazines. Stuart pointed to a black-and-white picture of a semi-nude woman with hundreds of piercings all over her face and torso. She was expressionless. Francis feigned interest, managed a "Whoa!" and walked outside for air.

The rain and wind slackened for a moment. Peeking back inside the door, Francis tried to redirect the expedition. "Hey, c'mon, let's check out the pawnshop."

John and Stuart looked at him. A moment passed. John wanted to make sure he was in charge of this day's activities. Then he broke the silence as Francis waited uncomfortably in the doorway. "Sure, man, let's check it out."

"That place was wicked," rapped Stuart as they walked. "I think I'm gonna do my tongue, maybe an eyebrow, too." Stuart thought of Amber and her bejeweled belly button.

Amber had a way about her that drew people close. Of course, an angelic face, eye-popping body, and sparkling tummy attracted plenty of male attention, but Amber also had a warmth that made her a sister any boy would love. There was the day at school when scrawny Stuart, teased just for being different, made the mistake of fighting back. He was promptly beaten to a pulp.

When he came home a bloody mess, Amber was there to mend his wounds and tell him jokes. Then, instead of heading off to her job as a cocktail waitress where she would have made a few hundred dollars, she called in sick and took Stuart to a local surf shop to buy him a pile of clothes she could scarcely afford. Money didn't matter; her little brother did. Because he was the poorest kid at The Academy, Amber figured Stuart needed cool clothes so he would fit in.

John listened to Stuart's piercing plans without interest, and turned to Francis, who walked one step behind. "So the 'rents let you out. They're pretty chill, huh?" He knew they were divorced and something about Peter's surfing exploits.

Francis replied, "Yeah, Dad's in town for a while. Then he'll leave for a couple of years. It just feels weird."

"Sorry, man," John offered, with his best attempt at genuineness.

"Yeah, sorry," added Stuart, not understanding what the big deal was, since he'd love it if his stepdad left. He opened the glass door, and the bell rang announcing their entry into the pawnshop.

They walked straight to the back wall where a locked gun case held a Remington 30/30 rifle, a Browning 12-gauge over-and-under shotgun, a Winchester, and a host of .22 caliber rifles. Then Stuart pointed to the semiautomatic big-game rifle on the end. "Whoa, check it out! BDDDDDDD … BAP, BAP … BDDDDDDD."

Looking at Stuart with mild disdain, John eased over to the pistol case, which was flanked by two knife cases. Francis went over to the assortment of dinged-up surfboards displayed in the front window. They spent the rest of the adolescent afternoon checking out and talking about every strange thing they could, including life at home. By dinnertime each boy was back home.

That evening, the phone rang next to Peter's still-aching head. "Hello? Yes, he is. Sure," he groaned, "Francis—phone."

Francis came down the steps. "Who is it?"

"Young lady," he said, rubbing his forehead and grimacing.

Francis took the cordless and ran into the next room. He caught his breath. "Hello?"

"Hi, Francis. How are you?" asked Summer's sweet voice.

"Fine."

"Sooooo … what's up?"

"Not too much. Hung out with Stuart and John on The Strip."

Surprised, Summer did not want to seem too interested. "So, what did you guys do?"

"Stuart talked a lot about his sister. She has sex right next to his room with some guy, and his stepdad doesn't care. He imitates the noises they make. He acts like it's all a big joke. I felt really sad for him. And I almost got sick right there in the tattoo place, looking at some girl with about a million piercings."

"That's gross," she said.

"Stuart's life seems so miserable. I don't know how he does it."

Summer didn't either. "So, what else did you guys do?"

"Oh, we hung out at the arcade, played some video games. Man, John is really into this one called "Sniper." He got the highest score and had all the free game tokens, so we played that for a while."

"What else?"

"When we were at the pawnshop, he kept checking out the pistols. They wouldn't let him touch one, but he asked all these questions. Seemed like he knew what he was talking about. I guess it's just strange he's into all that stuff—you know, war games, body piercing." He paused. "I don't think he'd actually get a piercing, though; I think his dad would go nuts if he pierced something. I don't know about Stuart."

Francis didn't want to talk about John or Stuart anymore. "Promise to keep a secret?" Francis asked.

"Promise."

"Went surfing before the folks got up. Totally awesome. The current pushed me at least a mile—really intense."

"Isn't that dangerous?"

"For some reason, I wasn't scared. I just wanted one good ride. Nothing else mattered."

"I think you're crazy." Summer laughed nervously but felt a strange new attraction to him. "And I'm not sure you should hang around those guys. Something's not right there."

When Francis didn't respond, Summer felt concern.

"I've got an idea," she offered. "Mom and Dad asked if I thought you'd come to church with us. I told them I didn't think you went much. But, well, what do you think? You want to go to church with us in the morning?" She wanted to give Francis a chance to know Jesus as she did.

"Sure," Francis answered without hesitation. Anything to be close to her.

"We'll pick you up at 10:45."

"Okay." As the cliché goes, the Lord works in mysterious ways.

The prior day's foul weather gave way to a brilliant blue Sunday. Outside, billowy clouds drifted by lazily, intermittently eclipsing the vivid sun. Inside, Francis, along with Summer's family, sat in the front row of the auditorium-like chapel where the heavens seemed to open on this vibrant day.

The preacher implored his audience, "There's a question we all must ask ourselves today, and your answer will surely shape your lives forever. Is life miraculous, or is it just, well, life? Are we in the midst of a great miracle given to us by God? Now, I must challenge each of you this morning to look at yourselves squarely and answer the question. If your answer is "This is no miracle," then you do not believe in the God of miracles. Perhaps you believe we are here by some cosmic chance, a one-in-a-trillion melding of mud and bio-chemistry. On the other hand, if you answer yes, then you do believe in the God of miracles. Ah, this moment is such a gift. Can you feel it? Can you feel it?"

Pastor Christopher Magiani was just getting warmed up. As he raised his hands, the congregation stood, some raising one hand, others two. Some had their arms outstretched, palms upward, eyes closed. Others reached high and cocked their heads back, their eyes wide open as if seeing Heaven itself.

"Alleluia!" cried one.

"Amen!" started a young man. "Yes, I feel it!"

Summer, her little brother, Steve, and her parents stood, hands in the air, swaying with the growing wave. Crying people walked up to the altar directly in front of Francis and the Overtons and knelt, faces to the floor.

Francis had never been to such a church. His mother had taken him to the nearby Methodist church for holidays, a few weddings, and his grandmother's funeral. But this church was of the charismatic variety where altar calls and healings were an expected weekly occurrence. The service usually lasted two and a half hours, and at the end the pastor would invite believers to come up to lay hands on one another, casting out demons or encouraging someone on a mission to Nicaragua.

Pastor Magiani cried out, "I see miracles all around me!" Then he opened his arms wide, as a mother hen would stretch out her wings to protect her flock of chicks.

"Praise God!"

"Amen! Yes, Jesus!"

"God is paying you a visit this morning," he continued in a softer voice, as if telling a secret. "He's knocking at your door, louder than ever this morning!" Louder, "Can you hear His knocking?"

"Yes, I can hear it!" cried out one man.

"Can you hear Him? What, you can't hear Him knock? You don't hear Him calling? Then see the demon that covers your ears! It's him, the Evil One! He keeps you from hearing!"

"I can hear Him now!" cried someone from the back of the room. Others came forward, weeping, and fell face-down on the floor next to the stage.

"Yes! You see Satan in the way! Tell him to move aside! Let God in and kick Satan out! Kick him out... NOW!" the pastor cried even louder. He paused, and then spoke softly, almost a whisper, "Now, can you hear the knocking?"

"Yes! Yes, I hear!" came a cry from the back of the chapel.

"Are you going to answer? Or are you going to leave God out in the cold?"

"No! Come in, sweet Jesus!" cried the man.

"Then get up! Open that door! Let Jesus in. Can you see the miracle? Open your eyes!"

Suddenly, the enraptured congregation and the pastor hushed. A young boy fell to the carpet and lay motionless on his back. It was Francis. Bill and Rose gasped. Summer was on her knees next to him first. She held him in her arms as Bill, Rose, and little Steve looked on. The congregation remained silent.

"Francis, Francis!" Summer called. Dazed, Francis awoke, looked up at her, and felt the warmth and comfort of her hand on his.

The pastor dropped to one knee. "Francis, I'm Pastor Magiani. Can you hear me?"

"Uh-huh, yes."

"What happened?" Bill asked, looking down at the pastor. "Should we call a doctor?"

"No," answered Pastor Magiani."

The pastor leaned down and said softly, "Francis, you are in church. Do you know what happened to you just now?"

Francis paused, then spoke haltingly, "Uh, you were asking... uh, if I could see Jesus. Everything went black. Then I had this dream. I was standing on a rock in the middle of a stormy sea with clouds rushing by. But there was no wind, no sound, and I wasn't afraid. For some reason, I was safe, and the waves couldn't touch me. Did I pass out?"

"You had a vision," the pastor concluded, then raised his voice and held his hands high, turning to the entranced congregation. "This young man has had a vision! He was standing on a rock in a stormy sea, but he was not afraid! Is that right, son?"

Now, as if drawn by an invisible force, some parishioners moved into the aisles or stood in front of their pews shaking fervently, speaking in a language Francis had never heard. They heaved, murmured, mumbled, and yelped.

"Yes," answered Francis quietly, nervously looking around.

The pastor leaned down to Francis and asked, "Do you know Jesus?" A few more folks nearby began speaking in tongues, praising, and worshipping.

"He's the Son of God, right?" answered Francis awkwardly, still nervously looking around.

The pastor looked straight into Francis' eyes. "Was he with you on that rock?"

"He must have been, or I would've been scared."

Now, it seemed everyone in the church was chanting, singing, and praising.

"Do you believe in Him . . . Jesus, the Son of the Almighty? Do you believe he saved you in that raging torrent that was in your vision?" asked the pastor, raising his voice to the heavens.

Francis looked around. The pastor put the microphone to Francis' mouth and waited. "Yes, Jesus saved me," answered Francis plainly.

The pastor turned to the audience and hollered, "Yes, amen! Jesus saved this boy!" Then he proceeded to his pulpit.

Bill followed the pastor up the steps and grabbed him by the arm before he could return to the lectern. "Are you sure he's okay?"

Pastor Magiani turned to the congregation as Bill let go. "This boy is fine! He's better than ever!"

Then he turned to Bill and Rose and said, "He has just had an event."

"A what?"

"An event. He's been touched by God."

"Praise Jesus!" Rose cried.

The congregation cheered; above the din came intermittent outbursts of "Lord Jesus!"

"Glory to God!"

"Thank you, Jesus!"

"Praise God!"

"Francis," the pastor asked softly, looking down from the stage, "can you stand?"

"I think so."

"Then lift him up!" the pastor cried for all to hear. The Overtons lifted Francis to his feet.

"Praise Jesus, the rock of salvation and truth! Let's move mountains! I can see miracles!" Magiani ran about the stage praising, worshipping, and speaking in tongues.

The congregation erupted into applause and spilled into the aisles. The Overtons, minus Summer, sang and praised along with them, while Francis, slouched in his seat, looked up at the ceiling and wondered what had happened. Summer rubbed his shoulders and neck as he faded in and out.

By the time the Overtons got him to their home, Francis had regained his composure. "How do you feel?" Bill asked.

Francis sat on the couch, and Rose brought him an orange juice. Summer held his hand.

Francis again told what happened. "I was standing on a rock in the middle of a storm, but the wind wasn't blowing, and the waves couldn't reach me. It seemed so real. And clouds rushed by me. I was in the clouds, but safe on this weird rock. Then I saw your faces and felt scared—you all looked so worried. But I'm okay. Don't worry."

Bill, who knew he had to explain what had happened to Peter and Anne, did not look forward to driving to the Kahne household. Rather than mince words, he decided, as he turned onto Francis' street, that it was best to tell it straight out.

Peter answered the door, surprised to see Bill and Summer instead of just his son. Bill wasted no time. "Hello, there. Well, Peter, there's something that happened with Francis in church today. I mean, it was quite a day. Wish you and Anne had been there for it. Yes, it was a day of miracles for everyone. I mean, if you didn't get a miracle, then you just weren't listening. People were falling in the aisles. The worship was like I've nev—"

These were more words than had ever passed between Peter Kahne and Bill Overton. Peter interrupted Bill's rambling. "What are you talking about? Something happened to Francis?"

Bill decided to get to the point, again. "Well, the pastor called it an event. You see, Francis had a vision from God, and, based on what he described so vividly, he was protected by His—that's God's—power."

"And he said Jesus protected him," added Summer.

"Vision?" Peter was stupefied.

"Well, he fainted. Now don't wor—"

"What! Fainted? You're kidding me, right?" Anger welled in Peter, thinking that the Overtons, who had seemed merely religious minutes ago, were now full-blown wackos who had gotten his son mixed up in some kind of religious cult.

"Don't worry, Peter, he's fine," Bill answered, being as calm as possible.

Then Francis interjected, "Dad, I'm okay. Mr. Overton's right, don't worry. I'm just a little tired."

Peter pulled Francis in the door and leaned toward Bill, pointing his finger. "He'd better be okay, or I'm heading over to that church and tearing it down with my bare hands."

Raising his palms in defense, Bill tried to reassure Peter. "Now, I know you're upset, but really, he's okay."

"He'd better be." Then Peter slammed the door on Summer and Bill. Francis was already on his way upstairs.

Late the next morning, Francis was still sleeping. Worried, Peter and Anne went up to his bedroom. To their horror, he lay in bed, snow white, eyes closed. A tear touched his pillow. He looked dead.

"Francis, Francis…wake up!" Peter and Anne shook him frantically.

Francis could hear them off in the distance, far, far away, and could feel the shaking, but it was as if someone else were being shaken. Francis was somewhere else.

※

Francis sat cross-legged on the bleached sand, wearing an oversized white T-shirt, baggy white pants, and unlaced white Keds. The sun was white, its warmth everywhere. It comforted him. Overhead, a steady breeze blew the same billowy clouds he had seen the previous morning, except this time they drifted offshore like a parade of lambs wandering away to parts unknown. He stretched out his arms overhead and could almost touch them. Then the wind blew even harder as the clouds rushed by faster. Waves rose higher, then crested as their giant liquid cavities fiercely sprayed water through tubes parallel to the shore. The huge, wind-whipped faces lurched toward the beach, curling down the shoreline as far as Francis could see. Then, from the steady rumble of the surf—

"Francis. Francis." The sound of his name was almost indistinguishable from the wind and waves.

"Listen."

Francis looked out over the water. He could barely make out the whispered words, "Francis, Francis. Do not be afraid."

Francis looked upward and all around. The voice repeated, "Francis. Francis. Francis."

Startled, Francis asked, "Where are you?"

From the waves the voice said, "Here."

"I can't see you."

"Here." Now the voice came from up and down the beach.

"But I can't see you!" Francis hollered.

"Listen."

Francis could now hear the voice clearly above the pounding of the waves and the rush of the wind. The waves seemed to pulse at a pace that matched the rhythm of his heartbeat.

"Hello! Hello!" cried Francis, turning his head frantically. He felt an invisible force striking his chest to the beat of his heart. He stood and walked into the water until it was over his head. Submerged, he noticed that the beating of his heart continued as the current carried him. Then he rose, now bobbing. Oddly, the sensation, while entirely unnatural, calmed him.

Instantly, he found himself back on the sand, soaking wet. But now the huge waves striking the shoreline were silent, just as the throbbing in his chest disappeared.

Turning his back to the sea, Francis could see the dunes aglow as flames leapt skyward. Embers floated overhead and fell into the sea. Behind the fiery dune, he could see his house. It too was on fire. He jumped up and ran through the inferno, stumbled and fell face-down in the soft sand, got up, and went down yet again. Through the intense heat of the blaze, he gazed at the second floor of his house and saw his parents wave to him from the balcony. They smiled as if nothing were happening. The house burned brightly but was not engulfed.

"Francis, turn and look to the sea," said the voice.

Standing in the fire, he slowly turned from his home and parents. The sun reflected across the wild waters as far as his squinting eyes could see. Scanning the gleaming waves, he almost had to turn away. Then the voice returned.

"Awaken."

Back in Francis' bedroom, Peter and Anne started to panic. "Francis, we're here. It's Mom and Dad! Wake up, son!" Peter begged.

"Francis, honey, it's Mommy. Please open your eyes!"

Peter put his hand over Francis' mouth and felt only the slightest breath. He grabbed the boy's shoulders and rattled him. Francis' mouth gaped, and his head snapped back and forth. His eyes rolled back, then slowly opened.

"Francis! My baby! You're awake! Thank God!" cried his mother.

Holding him, Peter's eyes pooled, remembering when he'd last cradled his boy as a baby so many years before. "Francis, what happened?"

"Am I home? What's going on? Why'd you wake me up?" Francis asked groggily.

"Why? You were barely breathing and white as a sheet, that's why!"

Francis looked up at his distressed parents, then looked beyond them, out the window. Light streamed in, filling the room. He felt a strange chill, as though he had stepped into a cool room after being out in a hot summer's day. His heart thumped so loudly he could actually hear the swishing of blood passing through it. Whatever had happened, Francis knew that other boys were not fainting in church or having dreams that rendered them nearly comatose. And, for the first time since he was a small child, Francis remembered the comfort his family gave him. He smiled.

"Let's get you up, son," Peter offered.

They pulled back the covers to help him out of bed. He slowly rose and put on his slippers, then shuffled down the hall to the bathroom. Peter and Anne followed.

"I'll be down for breakfast in a few minutes," said Francis. Then he closed the door to the bathroom and turned on the shower.

When Francis finally came downstairs, Anne had scrambled eggs and toast waiting. As she went to the refrigerator, Francis began. "Mom, Dad, I love you."

Tears welled in Anne's eyes as she poured the OJ, and she said, "Your father and I love you very much, too."

"I'd sure like to know what happened," barked Peter, still ready to raise hell at an evangelical church.

"I'm not exactly sure, but I know it all started when I passed out in Summer's church, and—"

"What started? What do you mean, son?" said Peter, increasingly impatient.

"It's like someone is telling me something, only I can't hear exactly what it is … like it's there, but I can't see it. And, I'm supposed to listen."

"To what?" Peter was now both concerned and annoyed.

"That's just it, Dad. I don't know for sure."

"What's the matter, honey?" Anne felt his brow with the back of her hand. "You seem a little warm. Maybe you have a fever." She opened the kitchen cabinet and pulled out a thermometer.

"I'm not sick, Mom."

"Well, I'm going to check, anyway." She slipped the thermometer into his mouth. Peter huffed and stuck his nose back in the paper.

"It's 98.6. You're fine." Anne, now satisfied, went about the kitchen, doing the dishes and putting away food.

Then the phone rang.

Anne answered, "Hello."

"Is Francis there?"

"Who's calling?"

"Stuart."

Francis took the call. After he hung up, he asked if he could go surfing with Stuart and John. A relieved Peter saw this as something totally normal. He practically kicked the boy down to the garage and helped him choose his board.

Once Francis was on his way, Peter came in to share with Anne a change of plans. "I've been thinking, maybe I'll wait a little while before heading back to the Left Coast. The surf's been decent for a change around here, and there are still a bunch of friends I haven't seen. There's a little bungalow down the street I could rent for a few weeks, so I won't be in the way around here. I want to hang with Francis a little longer, too. To be honest, I'm a little worried about him."

Anne's half smile belied the full one she felt. "Peter, if you want to stay longer, that's great. You know Francis loves having you around. And you don't have to find a place; you can stay here. Really, it's no problem."

"Anne, you're a sweet lady," he said, exercising just enough restraint to keep himself from running over and hugging her.

With that, Peter's visit had turned into the prospect of an entire summer with friends and a chance to really get to know his son. As the days unfolded, the one constant was surfing. Peter surfed with his buddies while Francis surfed with his. Sometimes they would run into one another on the five-mile stretch of beach that was theirs, or if they wanted to, catch a swell together behind Anne's house.

≋

Then, one morning, the phone rang at John's earlier than usual. "'Sup, dude?" Stuart greeted jokingly.

"Stuart, what are you doing up so early?" yawned John.

"Wanna hit The Strip?"

"Nah." While they were talking, John got up from his bed, walked into his father's office, and sat at the desk, fiddling with a huge ring of keys. Nicholas was still sound asleep from a late night at the restaurant.

"So what's goin' on, you doin' somethin' today?" asked Stuart, wondering what the strange jingling was in the background.

John said curtly in a hushed voice, "I'm busy. And you called too early, dude. Your sister making noises again?" Then he imitated the sex noises that Stuart had described to him, "Uh, uh, uh, oh, oh—"

"Cut it out! My stepdad woke me up when he got home from work," Stuart whined, not liking it when John teased him.

"Well, that doesn't mean you need to wake up everybody else. My dad's probably up now because of you. And I'm trying to open his office drawer."

There were at least twenty keys on his father's ring. One was the key to the file drawer. John flipped through them, trying the ones that appeared to fit.

"That's the one," said John under his breath.

"What are you doing?" Stuart asked with increasing curiosity.

The drawer slid open smoothly. The snub-nosed .38 and a box of shells lay at the bottom. The pistol looked smaller than John remembered. He picked up the piece and brought it close to his face, examining it from all angles. He could feel his temples pulse as he turned the pistol this way and that, marveling at the ease and quickness with which he could point it in all directions.

"What are you doing in your dad's office?" Stuart repeated.

"Listen to this." John put the phone up to the revolver and spun the cartridge. Click, click, click, click.

"What's that?"

"A .38."

"A pistol!"

"Yes."

"Whoa, crazy! Let's shoot it, dude!"

John did not want to share the weapon with Stuart or anybody else. He put the gun in his pocket, grabbed the box of bullets, and locked the drawer.

"No, that's stupid," said John smugly. "I thought you were smart."

"Aw, man, c'mon let's—"

"I said no, man," finished John flatly.

"Well, then, let's check out the jetty or something. It should be good after the storm. C'mon by, and we'll go before the tourists take over."

"Okay, but I'm going to crash for a while. Call me later." John hung up the phone and returned to his room, but he couldn't sleep.

He sat on his bed, looking down at his new toy. It felt light in his hands. Nicholas never went in that office drawer, so John figured he could keep the gun and shells hidden somewhere and his father would never know. He decided to hide it for a little while in the shoebox full of junk and old family pictures on the top shelf of his closet. After hiding the gun, he crept down the dusky hallway past his parents' bedroom. Nicholas was still asleep from ouzo and a late night at the restaurant. John's mother was in the kitchen making pastries for a church bake sale; on such occasions she cooked for what seemed like days at a time. The sweet smell filled the house as it had so many times before.

John called Stuart to tell him he was on his way, then grabbed his board from the basement. He started his ride fifty blocks southward.

The gray haze of the July sky weighed on him like a hot, wet shroud. Stuart lived a few miles off the beach, next to a trailer park and an adult bookstore. Leaving his spartan four-bedroom brick home several blocks west of the beachfront, John rode through the car-lined neighborhoods on his beach cruiser. He passed families loaded down with every manner of beach paraphernalia; couples holding hands and a six-pack cooler; single, forty-plus women carrying romance novels; and adolescents with skim boards. They all walked, trance-like, along the street, heading to the soon-to-be boiling sands of the beach.

He passed beautifully manicured North Beach mansions and pristine white condos where the traffic medians were lined with lush pink oleander. Just ahead, along Beachstreet, stretched forty blocks of concrete, asphalt, and a billion dollars per year of commerce. He passed Nick's without notice, looping down to the paved boardwalk where the black, paint-striped bike trail stretched north and south. Delirious tourists, overcome by the ether of the "big beach" and the endless ocean, wandered into his path. He brushed by them, almost running them over without slowing down.

At Beach Boulevard he turned off the trail and headed westward past the bustling Dairy Queen, a pizza place on the corner, and, a half block farther west, the piercing and tattoo parlor he and his buds frequented. A row of abandoned restaurants, bars, and apartments lined both sides of the street, along with two clubs where, evenings most summer weekends, hip-hoppers either paid the $30 entry, or lingered in the streets, partying and causing their special brand of mayhem. It was not uncommon for gunshots and knife fights to erupt, unbeknownst to mamas who pushed babies in strollers, and papas who carried little ones on their shoulders just a few blocks away.

Politicians labeled these problems "crowding." Whatever it was, it reminded many resort business folks of the time, years ago, when college frat kids didn't feel too welcome on the snow-white sands along the resort, so they organized a little get-together not soon forgotten. Colleges up and down the East Coast and beyond advertised the party. A flood of 50,000 students, each seemingly with an attitude, surged through the streets and overloaded the 10,000 hotel rooms. Merchants braced. Safely sequestered at the station in riot gear, outnumbered police prepared for the worst. Street peddlers sold T-shirts with Malcolm X pointing angrily and the slogan "It's a Black Thing... You Now Understand" in huge letters. Farrakhan fanatics passed out white hate leaflets on city corners. The family resort was about to mutate into a war zone.

What had started as some Labor Day weekend college fun turned into full-scale anarchy. Windows were broken, shops were looted, and hotel rooms were ransacked. Shattered TVs and chairs littered the streets and boardwalk. Revelers cleaned out 7-Elevens and climbed on top of overturned police cars. The insanity lasted until sunrise, when police from five neighboring cities plus the National Guard were called in to clear the streets of tuckered-out partiers and finally quell the uprising. Virginia Beach had hit the big time. The riots were broadcast on every news channel across all major news-wires. It was world news — and a public relations disaster.

In the following few years, business along the resort strip plummeted. The carefully crafted image of a family beach was replaced by a beach trying to shake a sordid past and find a new identity. Planners met and met and met. New committees were born. It seemed the more police cracked down on antisocial or criminal behavior, the worse things got. Amidst this climate was born the first good idea to hit the resort since beach music. Out of one of those new committees, a smart fellow offered a simple but ingenious proposal.

In response to repeated cries by angry business owners to crack more heads and make more arrests, he said, "Hey, why throw the baby out with the bathwater? Let's entertain the people we have walking the sidewalks every night and invite everybody to our shows. Let's call it Beachstreet USA."

Politicians bought the idea, and money was budgeted for dozens of strategically placed street performers on busy sidewalks, side streets, and parks to entertain folks on summer nights. It was a hit, and business started booming again. The beach was back with a bigger and bolder image. Families returned. But some businesses did not escape the fallout from the riots.

One of these was a little restaurant on a hot corner. A Greek family had owned and operated it for two generations. It was a clean, simple business that put bread on the table and kids through college. It also happened to sit in the way of secret but soon to be revealed plans to build an upscale hotel resort and retail complex. Without this corner, the mega-deal would not fly. City planners and developers commiserated. The only answer was to seize the prime property by capitalizing on new, permissive eminent domain and seizure laws. After all, the project would have a public parking garage! And so, despite a ruling by the circuit court outlawing the seizure of private property for reasons other than public safety, and after a years-long appeals battle that the Greeks could ill afford to fight, the property was sold to developers and the city for "fair" market value.

Now, it appeared a chaotic and deteriorating Beach Boulevard area might again spawn a round of civil unrest and public seizure. While large-scale riots seemed unlikely, an after-hours murder or two, along with some bad press, might require actions deemed necessary for the "public good." One such measure came preemptively in the form of a decree: public parking lots throughout the resort would be closed at midnight. Independently operated bar and club businesses suffered as unwitting, angry late-night patrons were turned away from the lots for which they paid taxes.

Developers salivated as new public-private partnership opportunities unfolded before their eyes. Farther north, plans were already underway by those in cahoots to help John's father out of business. But this was of no concern to John. By the time he had reached the tiny three-bedroom with the overgrown yard, he was drenched with sweat and dying to get into the water. Leaning his bike against the run-down house, he pushed the doorbell. When it did not work, he knocked four equally spaced times, intoning another day of hanging out with Stuart and checking out the surf.

Stuart and John grew even closer as the sweltering summer headed into August. Occasionally, Francis would be included if there was some surf to be had. But since he had gotten queasy on their last outing to the tattoo parlor, excursions to The Strip to check out weird stuff were left to Stuart and John.

8. A Legend

"WHAT'S GOOD?" began Stuart excitedly, not expecting an answer. "Get a look at the waves yet? Looks real rideable. You wanna meet down at the jetty and check it out?"

"Yeah, saw them earlier. Okay, the jetty sounds good," answered Francis.

"Be down there in an hour." Stuart hung up and looked over at John who was kicked back on the stained, tan La-Z-Boy in Carl's den, soaking up the air conditioning and glued to his porn. Stuart smirked and said, "That's disgusting. You know, sometimes Dad leaves it on when he goes to bed, and that's what I see first thing in the morning. I don't think other kids have these problems."

John shrugged. "My dad wouldn't know what porn is. He's just a basic cable guy. I think it was taboo or something in Greece."

Back at the Kahne garage, Francis prepared to head down to the surf spot. He picked out his board and loaded it on the side carriage of his bike.

"Don't be too late, and be careful," called Anne, her standard last words whenever Francis left for anything. Francis pedaled down the driveway and turned left toward the jetty, located at the southernmost point of the boardwalk.

Once past the cottages and condos that packed the North Beach landscape, Francis veered left onto the concrete boardwalk extending forty blocks southward, ending at a pile of rocks that protects Rudee Inlet. These enormous rocks reach over 200 feet into the sea on either side of the inlet, causing sand to accumulate under the waves and creating a break desirable for surfers. Just south of the inlet emerges a high-density seaside neighborhood named after the Croatan Indians who once thrived there. Unlike old, established North Beach, Croatan blossomed from just a few houses thirty years ago, to rows of million-dollar-plus, three-story homes that border Lake Rudee to the north and west and Camp Pendleton National Guard base to the south. Here, officers vacationed, prisoners awaited trial, and amphibious maneuvers occurred with a frequency annoying to the nearby nouveau riche. Just a few miles farther west beyond Rudee Inlet and its winding, marshy tributary known as Owl Creek, emerges another base, Oceana Naval Air Station, where "top guns" practice touch-and-goes and dummy runs in state-of-the-art fighter jets.

Oceana has been around since the 1940s, when Virginia Beach was a sleepy town of farms and two-lane roads winding from North Carolina to the Chesapeake Bay and inland to Norfolk. Where once prop planes and jets of lower decibels flew over farms, forests, and desolate beaches, now ear-piercing F-18s buzzed wealthy ocean-front property owners sitting on their decks sipping the latest over-oaked California Chardonnay. For good measure, on the way back to base and after a loop over the ocean, pilots kicked on the after-burners above tourists baking on the packed beaches and elderly golfers enjoying a "quiet" round at the nearby, very private Princess Anne Country Club.

Francis approached the north jetty. It was close to noon and the beach was already jammed. Toddlers frolicked in ankle-deep water under the watchful eyes of mothers. A lifeguard would occasionally blow her whistle when anyone ventured too far offshore. A stiff breeze blew up the swell, and chest-high surf pounded tourists who attempted to bodysurf or boogie board.

There would be no surfing on this side of the inlet—too many tourists—so Francis turned toward the Rudee Bridge, which connected The Strip to the residential section where Croatan's residents enjoyed dominion over pseudo-public beaches. He pedaled into the neighborhood, rode down Croatan Road, then cut through Virginia Dare and down to the area of the jetty where waves might be had without a thousand vacationers. Other bikes, some with surfboard racks, were locked to the chainlink fence. Francis rode to the top of the dirt hill that overlooked the beach, and saw Stuart and John near the water, each with his board tucked under his arm, searching for perfect waves. The waves looked rideable, but they were smaller than the break on the other side of Rudee. For several minutes the boys seemed frozen in time. Then, Stuart and John turned and started walking away from the water toward Francis.

"Hey, bud!" hollered Stuart as he approached. "Let's try Pendleton."

With little else said, the three headed south to Camp Pendleton in hope of bigger surf. The noon sun scorched the pavement as phone lines hummed. Two F-18s flying low and hard, straight from Oceana, screamed over their heads and headed out to sea, only to loop back farther north over thousands of tanning tourists, then down to base for another touch-and-go. The bike ride took five minutes. As the boys rode through the gate and down to the water, they noticed an unusually big swell kicking up. They had happened upon the best waves of the season. It was like a scene from the movie *The Endless Summer.*

Local legends were on hand. Wes Laine had dusted off his board and come out to prove he still ruled the local break after twenty-five years. Native Harry Heinke, visiting from his new residence in Costa Rica, was in the water, his long, silver mane glistening in the sun as he paddled after a head-high wave. The most renowned of all, gray-haired Pete Smith, wearing a faded Pete Smith's Surf Shop T-shirt, sat cross-legged under an umbrella, overseeing the occasion. He was the man who had practically put Virginia Beach on the world surfing map by opening the first local surf shop and promoting the pastime as a sport. The boys were in awe.

As they walked down to the water, another local legend bobbed from behind a swell, sitting upright on his board. It was Peter. He glanced toward the boys, then quickly turned, dropped to his stomach, and began to paddle into the path of an overhead swell. The wave pulled him up to it like a mother's arms pulling her child to her breast. Peter slashed across the face of the wave, shredding it to pieces.

It was all just too much for the three boys. They looked at each other, gave out a yell, jumped in, and paddled through the perfect sets to find their own waves. Peter watched his son and his two friends pop "ollies" and rip it all up and down the Pendleton beach. Once he nodded to Francis. Francis smiled and waved back. No words needed to be spoken.

Off in the distance, a dark cloud hung unnoticed, low against the horizon. As the day wore on, however, it became apparent the cloud was a storm heading in from the nearby Eastern Shore. Most of the other surfers left, including Peter. Undaunted, the boys surfed until the wind kicked up and their arms couldn't paddle anymore. Soon, the clouds gathered over North Beach, the breeze stiffened, and the glassy waves turned to mush. The beach emptied, leaving the boys with long bike rides.

Stuart lumbered home in the beginnings of an electrical storm. He arrived to a front yard full of cars and SUVs. The sounds of loud music, strange male voices, and what sounded like his giggling sister greeted him.

On the other side of the beach, lightning cracked and thunder rolled as John rode back to his house and the aromas of his mother's cooking. It was quiet inside. Nicholas was at the restaurant, preparing for the early dinner rush. The gun was safe in the shoebox.

While Francis pedaled homeward, Anne headed out with the girls to drink champagne at their favorite haunt, a wine bar where girls can be girls without being hit on by a burnt-out surfer or some jerk wearing a ball cap.

Peter had driven back to the empty house and showered. He downed a few beers and ate some leftovers, then trudged upstairs to the guestroom to crash, reminding himself that he was only a guest.

Francis sped home as large raindrops pelted his back and lightning flashed repeatedly nearby. It seemed to follow him. Thunderheads mounted over the water. He turned left off the concrete boardwalk and then right toward North Beach, just missing a woman carrying an umbrella and a beach bag. He pedaled faster as the rain intensified. Lightning crackled. A strike hit a tree one block behind him. The huge boom and a fountain of sparks frightened him so badly he almost fell off his bike. Swerving right, he momentarily lost control, then sharply veered left to regain his balance. Finally, drenched and exhausted, Francis pulled into the driveway.

Then, CRACK...BOOM! Lightning blasted the transformer just above him. A surge of heat knocked him off his bike and into his mother's garden next to the Annie's Garden sign Peter had given her when they first bought the house. The transformer was ablaze. Severed wires buzzed and crackled, whipping in the street like insane snakes. Sparks flew everywhere. A loose wire dangled inches from Francis' face. His eyes were wide open. The voice returned.

"Francis, get up."

He slowly rolled over. Everything was sizzling and popping.

"Get up."

Francis got up, but didn't back away from the undulating high-voltage wire that now appeared to be the source of the voice.

Peter came bursting out the door. He stumbled through the garden toward Francis, who stood, smoking, on the lawn next to his shattered surfboard.

"Francis!"

Francis stood silently staring at the dancing wire inches away.

"Good God!" Peter ran across the yard and dove, knocking Francis to the ground, rolling him over and out of reach of the hissing wire.

Peter grabbed his boy by the shoulders. He lifted him up and looked him square in the eyes. "Francis! You okay, son? You okay? Say something!"

Thinking Francis had his legs under him, Peter let go for a moment. Francis went down in a heap. Smoke and steam rose from him as he hit the ground. Peter reached into his pocket and dialed 9-1-1.

They waited. Peter rocked his boy, who lay limply in his arms, staring upward. Francis' eyes remained open. Finally, sirens wailed in the distance and got louder.

The paramedics huddled around him. They shone a light in his eyes and held up fingers to find out if he could count, or even see, for that matter. Peter watched anxiously.

"Is he going to be okay?" he asked, choked up.

A young paramedic looked over his shoulder and answered with more than a small measure of surprise, "Actually, there are no visible burns. His tennis shoes and the rubber tires of his bike probably saved him." Then he added, "The thing is, he's not speaking. His eyes are open, he seems awake, but he doesn't respond to questions."

They lifted Francis onto the stretcher and placed him in the ambulance. Gathering his wits, Peter asked before they drove off, "Can I ride with him?"

"Sure, just a moment," and they helped him into the emergency vehicle.

Once at the hospital, Francis was rushed through the emergency room doors to awaiting doctors. Peter could only linger in the lobby and pace. Later, after he repeatedly asked when he could go back to see his son, they let him through.

Peter walked anxiously down the winding, white halls to a partitioned bay, thankful that his son was not in intensive care. Francis lay peacefully, eyes closed. A middle-aged Hispanic nurse with a slight accent completed the process of affixing him to an array of monitors. Her nametag said Esmeralda.

She turned and said with a pleasant smile, "Are you his father?"

"Yes. Is he okay?"

"He's a strong young man. He will be fine," Esmeralda said without hesitation. Then she smiled broadly and walked over to Francis. She reached to his pale forehead and brushed his long locks away from his face. "Yes, he's just fine."

Then she turned to Peter and said, "The doctor will be here very soon. But you don't need to worry. Just sit here." She scooted a chair next to Francis' bed. "Oh, and where is his mother? I will make sure the admissions desk knows she's on the way, yes?"

"Uh, yeah, sure," he answered.

Esmeralda nodded and left the room.

Peter wanted desperately to reach Anne but didn't have her cell phone number. He had left her a voicemail in case she checked messages on the home phone.

After several minutes alone with a still-speechless Francis, Peter leaned to him. "Francis, it's Dad. Please say something."

Just then, Champagne Anne burst into the room. "Francis! My baby! It's Mama. I'm here. I'm here." She was drunk and she knew it. Touching Francis' forehead and brushing back his tasseled hair, she exclaimed, "Ohmygod! Ohmygod! Francis, I'm so sorry!"

Francis' eyes flickered. He looked straight at her and smiled. "Don't worry, Mama. I'm fine ... just real tired." And that was all he said. Then he shut his eyes and went to sleep, while Anne whimpered.

Peter and Anne cried over their boy until they fell asleep in the curtained cubicle. Nurses and doctors checked on Francis throughout the night. In the wee hours, Peter was awakened by a nudge on his shoulder. A doctor looked down at him with a smile. "Mr. Kahne, your boy is going to be okay. All his vitals look normal. You and your wife should go home and get some rest."

Anne stirred from the slight commotion, her head on Peter's shoulder, her arm resting on his. Her hair fell over her cheek and draped onto his chest. Looking down at her as she slept and softly breathed, he remembered their first date when they had passed out on her couch after a night of partying. For the first time since before the divorce, he remembered Annie.

"Anne. Anne, did you hear the doc? Annie, get up. Francis is fine. Let's go."

Still half asleep, she nodded wearily.

"We can come back in a few hours." He spoke in a hushed tone so as not to awaken him.

"No, we can't leave him here by himself," she pleaded.

Peter replied reassuringly, "Honey, he's fine. Look at him. He's sleeping like a baby."

Anne leaned over and kissed Francis. She winced as the result of too much Veuve Cliquot kicked in.

Peter kissed Francis on the forehead, took Anne by the arm, and they walked out of the room. As they went through the exit doors, Anne leaned on Peter, took his hand, and began to weep. Memories of their love and life together flashed through Peter's mind. Once outside, the quiet rain continued, interrupted by distant rumblings of thunder and flashes of lightning. Peter opened the door and gently helped her into the car. She cried as they drove silently down the empty streets. When they approached the house, the headlights illuminated the scorched street where live wires had writhed just hours before. The neighborhood was completely dark. The windows of the house were black.

Peter parked the car, then looked over to Anne, asleep, exhausted. He shook his head and smiled, remembering when they used to arrive home from late-night parties. He would walk around to her side of the car and ceremoniously carry her to the front door, fling it open with his foot, and whisk her across the threshold like it was their honeymoon all over again.

"Why not?" he muttered to himself, as he lifted her limp, slender body out of the car. She did not stir. Despite his sobriety, he stumbled a bit on the walkway and struggled up the steps to the doorway, almost dropping her. Somehow, he got the door open.

Once inside, Peter placed Anne carefully on the couch and hunted around for a flashlight. It was in the kitchen cabinet, right where he remembered. He stuffed it in his back pocket and proceeded to carry Anne up to her room. Peter dripped with sweat from the exertion and lack of air conditioning. He laid her on the dank, unmade sheets, slowly removed her shoes, and wrestled with her slacks, which seemed glued to her, finally removing them. The flashlight rested on the bedside table facing the bed. It cast a pool of yellow light over her glistening body. Peter paused. Her legs were still firm, maintained by hundreds of hours on the stationary bike and jogging with the girls.

Catching himself wandering to a place he knew he shouldn't go, he pulled the sheets over her, took the flashlight, and headed downstairs for a candle and some matches. He returned to her room and placed the flashlight on the table.

"Anne. Annie. Wake up," he whispered.

She stirred and opened her eyes sluggishly. Peter held the lit candelabra from the dining room table. "What are you doing?" she asked groggily.

"The power is out. Here's a flashlight if you need to get up."

"Is Francis okay?"

"Yes, he's fine. Just get some rest."

Peter left for the guestroom. The rain ebbed for a moment; then came a startling clatter. Peter quickly pulled back the curtain and saw golf-ball-sized hailstones bouncing in the yard. Spent, he blew out the candles and crumpled onto the bed without undressing.

≋

The events of the day roiled in his mind like the racket outside. After what seemed like restless hours, he finally drifted into a state of dreamy semi-consciousness. The hail turned into howling winds.

Peter found himself and a young woman speeding across choppy seas in an old wooden powerboat, one of those polished classics with sleek lines and a rounded windshield. To his horror, they were surrounded by waterspouts. Peter dodged, but the furious winds pulled the vessel closer. Each time, just when he thought they were going to be sucked up, he managed to steer away. Finally, in the distance, he saw an island with a cabin on its leeward side. He made a dash for it. Once there, they tied to a pole and walked across a gnarled wooden dock toward a slightly opened door from which glowed a sliver of light. At the door, Peter stopped, now carrying the woman, who suddenly looked a lot like Anne. The waterspouts returned, this time with faces of women he knew. Frozen with fear that he and Anne would be sucked into the sky, he was unable to step beyond the threshold. The light was just an arm's length away. As he stood at the doorway, petrified, the light flickered and began to fade.

≋

Peter awakened in a sweat, glued to the sheets. The air was stifling. Through the window shade, he could see muted bursts of light that nevertheless seemed to break the silence. He turned and tossed as flashbacks of the dream consumed him, until dawn, when he finally went back to sleep. A few minutes later, the clock radio blared and the air conditioner kicked on. Peter jumped, knocking the radio off the bedside. It continued to play.

His hand ripped the cord from the wall socket. The song stopped. The power was back.

9. Lightning Strikes Twice

John had made it home to his North Beach neighborhood without getting blasted by lightning. Once inside, he drifted silently through the kitchen. His mother looked up from her cooking, startled. Her drawn face glowed in the light of the gas range. Power outages did not stop her. She pleaded with John to sit and eat. He stopped for an instant, grumbled a "no thanks, Mom," went to his room, and locked the door. A few hours later, he heard Nicholas come home early from the restaurant and tell his wife how much business he had lost because of the outage.

As the candle flickered on the kitchen counter, Nicholas started, "People lined up to get in, an' then boom, everything go out. We wait for while. Then people leave to go ... I don't know where they go. But they go. We lose lotta money. You got matches round here? Where is Yannie? He home, I hope."

John tried to tune out his father, along with the sweltering heat. In the otherwise dead quiet of the house, the talk between his parents downstairs seemed to echo in his head. The more he tried to block them out, the louder they got, especially the thick, guttural, Greek voice of his father complaining about business. John hated it.

The next morning, when the power returned, John awakened

before his parents. He went into the kitchen and opened a Tupperware container full of his mother's sweet Greek delicacies. He filled a plate and poured a tall glass of milk, then sat alone in the den and watched the news channel his dad had been watching when power was last on.

Breaking News showed a well-produced, almost slick video of radical Muslims training to be terrorists, supposedly inside the United States or Mexico. They toted machine guns, wore what appeared to be pillowcases over their heads with holes for eye sockets, shot at human silhouettes, and dashed around an obstacle course like NFL players. The recording had been given to a reporter by an anonymous informant near the Mexican border. The reporter had been doing a story on illegal immigration, but when he played the message and heard the words of the scholarly English-speaking narrator, the story got much bigger and was broadcast around the globe.

"Deep in the heart of the Americas, Brothers of Islam train to eliminate the infidel. We see his evil, by the grace of Allah, and will destroy it. Brave fighters and martyrs rejoice! Praise be to Allah! Our time is here. See? We prepare to deliver the blow that will take the head of Satan and feed it to rabid dogs. Nowhere is safe for you. There will be no end to your torment. Infidels, we are at your doorstep. Martyrs who prepare for their rewards in heaven have entered your homeland. The final battle is very near. And we will be victorious on earth and in heaven. Praise be to Allah! *Allah hu Akbar!*"

Experts from Counterterrorism Headquarters in Langley, Virginia, called it a *fatwa,* declaring jihad, or holy war. The Brothers of Islam mentioned in the message was a worldwide Islamic organization that world opinion had previously deemed moderate. It now vaulted to the infamous level of Hamas, al Qaeda, and Hezbollah. According to terrorism experts, The Brothers of Islam had aligned itself with the Islamic Front, an alliance of Islamic nations. The overt association of the two groups indicated to many insiders a concerted desire to make "the Americas," or the United States of America, as it was interpreted by counterterrorism experts, an Islamic nation.

The harrowing words played on every news station. A flash scrolled across the bottom of the screen, noting that the president would deliver a speech that evening. Politicians and conservative radio talk-show hosts were interviewed about the need to strengthen border, port, and airport security. Others warned that we were headed for the end of days. One man preached how, in all of history, no nation's moral standards had fallen so far and so fast as those of the United States of America.

This evangelist told the story of Vietnam POW hero Jeremiah Denton's return to Norfolk during Operation Homecoming in 1973. After a stay of eight years at the prisoner of war camp popularly named the "Hanoi Hilton," including a bonus package of deprivation, torture, and captivity at the hands of the Vietcong, Denton returned to a starkly different America the Beautiful.

When he was captured in 1965, *The Sound of Music* won Hollywood's top honor, an Academy Award for best picture. In contrast, only a few years later and only halfway through his incarceration, the same honor went to none other than the X-rated *Midnight Cowboy* in 1969.

Then the preacher described another example of the radical change that took place during Denton's imprisonment. When US Navy Captain Denton arrived in Norfolk and was chauffeured with his wife through his hometown, he asked, "What do those neon signs with XXX mean?" His wife, embarrassed and ashamed, explained. Clearly, according to the man in the pulpit, the nation that Jeremiah Denton and many others had sacrificed so much for had fallen from grace.

A few years after his return, Denton wrote a book called *When Hell Was in Session,* telling the gut-wrenching story of his inhuman captivity, which coincided with America's decadent fall, marked by just a few turbulent years of protest and cultural revolution. Now, the preacher surmised that hell had reconvened in a new way, this time right here at home rather than in some faraway land. The United States seemed in the midst of a much different, much scarier, but equally rapid kind of revolution — and the comfortable consistencies of everyday life were disrupted by it.

John channel-surfed, watching in amazement as vehement protesters stopped the regularly scheduled *Today* show's live Pharrell interview and concert at Rockefeller Center with Matt Lauer and Al Roker. Instead of interviewing the critically acclaimed hip-hop star, Matt and Al interviewed protesters. Virginia Beach's hometown star, Pharrell, and his groupies would have to wait for another day.

Al and Matt deftly presided over the unusual events. Signs read STRENGTHEN OUR BORDERS; GLOBAL WARMING + HOMEGROWN TERRORISTS = WE'VE GOT BIG PROBLEMS; THE END IS NEAR; JESUS SAVES; and ALLAH BLESS AMERICA. The mood on the streets of New York approached full-scale panic. War had been declared inside our borders in plain English on a two-dollar DVD delivered by an anonymous man to a reporter somewhere in the Texas desert. John took another bite of baklava and kicked up his feet on the coffee table.

At the Hicks house, a hung-over boy stirred. The night before, Stuart had biked westward up Beach Boulevard, only a ten-minute ride from the Camp Pendleton surf spot. On the way, he stopped at Dairy Queen to pick up dinner to go: a Blizzard and a chili dog. As he rode homeward, the storm front descended and the sky turned dark. He could see lightning flashing over North Beach. Just a few blocks from home, he remembered that Carl was pulling a double shift and wouldn't return until sunrise.

In time to beat the heavy rain, Stuart noticed unfamiliar cars in his yard and down the street. Two shiny black Escalades practically blocked the front doorway. He could hear laughter and loud, thumping music. He squeezed between the cars and walked up to the door. His sister let loose a loud cackle as he entered. The house was full of people. Amber lounged on the couch with two gangster types. One had a single gold tooth, which sparkled in his broad white smile. The other, sporting a hip-hop grill, groped at her as she laughed and deftly swung her hair back over her shoulder. Stuart had walked into a full-scale party.

The night before, Amber had hooked up with a group of rappers from a club down on The Boulevard. Now they were her best friends. Most wore white baggy T-shirts and jeans. Many sported various gold-plated, silver, and cubic zirconium adornments. Stuart bumped his way through the sweaty crowd that seemed to sway to the hip-hop bass. The air was thick with the smell of cigarettes, beer, and marijuana.

Somehow he made his way to the kitchen and opened his bag of dinner. The sight and smell of food attracted a few of the more stoned gentlemen, who sat on either side of the boy as he licked his thick, chocolatey DQ Blizzard, which really required a spoon to eat. Stuart looked from side to side at each of them. Smartly, he reached into his bag and placed the greasy hotdog on the table. The two looked on longingly. Then, without pause, he reached into the kitchen drawer. He pulled out a long chef's knife. With one quick swipe, he chopped the dog down the middle. The two gentlemen jumped back, almost falling out of their seats. Stuart smiled and offered each a half. They laughed as only stoned people do, each devouring his portion in seconds.

One of the bleary-eyed fellows, after wiping his mouth with his sleeve, said, "You a-ight, man. Got some weed for the man if he wants?"

Stuart licked his Blizzard, turned to each of his new boys, and nodded. "Sure."

As the rain fell and the thunder rolled the partying intensified. The power stayed on in this dismal neighborhood, perhaps because few homes and no trailers had central air to draw on the load. So, the revelry raged on, drowning out the storm that pelted the tiny house. Young Stuart drank beers, which he had done before at Ramsey's, as well as on nights when dear stepdad was in the sharing mood. Stuart, however, had no previous measure to regulate his intake of marijuana, and hence toked enough for several fourteen-year-olds. The room swam, and everything stopped mattering, even the gun he saw protruding from someone's pocket. He partied with his new band of brothers until he could no longer laugh or keep his eyes open. The night ended quickly for him.

Stuart lay comatose until the early morning hours when he stirred for no apparent reason. The room was bright. Slumped in Carl's recliner, he shielded his eyes from the glaring light and groaned. After a few seconds, he realized he was actually in the den and had passed out. Stuart had achieved the worst headache of his life, the pain further amplified by the pervasive stench of stale beer and cigarettes, as well as the profanity-laced hip-hop tunes that still filled the room. Before he could even think about getting up, sickness welled up in him from his head to his stomach. As sweat began to bead on his brow, he upchucked over the side of the La-Z-Boy onto the filthy shag carpet.

"Oh, God!" Stuart was in agony. Barely able to see, he squinted, beginning to notice that the house was trashed and everyone had gone. The music pumped away, compounding the misery of the boy's first hangover. Droplets of puke hung on his chin. He rolled over and moaned some more, then slowly cranked the lever to elevate the chair. As he rose, the room spun like a merry-go-round. Steadying himself on the arm of the sofa, he headed toward the hallway bathroom. On the way he banged against every piece of furniture in his path. Finally, he lunged at the bathroom doorframe as if it were a rock in a rushing river. He made it to the sink and splashed his face, then wandered through the house to see who was left. The house was empty—his sister was gone.

≈

Despite the doctor's reassurance, Anne was worried. She felt, as only a mother can, that Francis wasn't entirely okay. After hanging up her bedside phone, she threw on a blouse and jeans. As she left her bedroom, she heard the clock radio go off in the guestroom, then a crash. The music alarm stopped.

Through the door, she asked, "Peter, you okay? I'm heading to the hospital. Do you want to come?"

"Uh, yeah. I'll be right out. Just give me a minute."

Inside of half an hour, they were walking into Francis' hospital room. He was awake and sitting up.

"Francis, son, it's good to see you. You feeling okay?" asked Peter optimistically.

Fully conscious and rested, Francis answered, "I'm fine, Dad."

Anne sat on the bed next to Francis and looked at him carefully. She touched his cheeks and forehead, and squeezed his arms and hands. "You feel a little warm. Are you sure you're okay?"

"Yes, I'm sure." He really did feel fine.

"When was the last time the doctors checked on you?" she asked.

"I'd like to go home, Mom. Let's go." As Francis started to get up, a doctor walked into the room. He was not the one who had checked on Francis overnight.

"Whoa, there, partner. That was quite a jolt you had last night. I'm not sure you're ready to be moving around."

As the doctor spoke, Francis walked to the bathroom and closed the door behind him.

"Well, I guess he is ready. Mr. and Mrs. Kahne, his vitals are normal and he has no burns or abrasions. I'm really surprised to say this, but it's almost as if he never was struck by lightning. As far as I'm concerned, you can take him home. All I can tell you is he's one lucky kid."

Francis emerged, walked to his neatly folded, singed clothing, and quietly began to dress. His shoes were black and tattered, the laces were splayed in every direction, but still he put them on. Then he went to the bed and sat waiting.

"I'll have a nurse roll over a wheelchair for you—hospital policy."

In a few minutes Francis' chariot arrived, and he was escorted out of the room and down the hallway by a Caribbean nurse with glassy green eyes. Peter and Anne followed. When they reached the exit, the nurse stopped and walked around to help Francis off the chair. When their eyes met, she stepped back in surprise.

"Lawdy, goodness, my little angel!" She clasped both her hands across her bosom and smiled joyfully. "I've never seen such a thing. Look at those pretty eyes. Why, they are just divine– yes, divine." She shook her head. "You take good care now, little man. Don't want to see ya back here again. Do ya hear what I'm tellin' ya?"

Francis smiled and nodded. Peter and Anne looked at each other curiously and shrugged their shoulders. While Peter went to get the car, the nurse, Francis, and Anne waited at the entrance. The nurse just laughed and shook her head as Anne and Francis got into the car and drove off into the brilliant morning.

Francis turned from gazing at the nurse. "I want to talk to Summer, Mom. Can I use your cell phone, please?"

After describing to Summer what had happened, Francis reassured her. "I'm fine. But it's weird getting struck by lightning. It didn't even hurt. Everything just stopped."

"Francis, can I come over to see you?" she asked excitedly.

"That would be great. What time?" Francis felt the adolescent rush that drew him to her.

"Mom's leaving now to go shopping. Can I come now?"

"Okay. See you in a little while."

Anne looked sternly at Francis. "Don't you think you should rest?"

"I feel fine, Mom. Stop worrying."

While Francis and Anne talked, Peter listened to the breaking news on the radio about the terrorist video and demonstrations in the streets of every major American city. Once home, Peter hurried to the TV and turned on CNN. One rock-star reporter had transferred from his embedded status in Iraq to the desert somewhere along the Mexican border where the video had been obtained. People suspected it had been made in Mexico, although no one was sure.

Clips showed hundreds of gun-toting militia in white hoods and tunics, supposedly Muslim funeral garb depicting preparedness for martyrdom. The audio repeated the ominous refrain: "Deep in the heart of the Americas, Brothers of Islam train to eliminate the infidel. We see his evil, by the grace of Allah, and will destroy it. Brave fighters and martyrs rejoice! Praise be to Allah! Our time is here. See. We prepare to deliver the blow that will take the head of Satan and feed it to rabid dogs. Nowhere is safe for you. There will be no end to your torment. Infidels, we are at your doorstep. Martyrs who prepare for their rewards in heaven have entered your homeland. The final battle is very near. And we will be victorious on earth and in heaven. Praise be to Allah! *Allah hu Akbar!*"

Peter and Anne were mesmerized by the TV, as were tens of millions of Americans. It was as if the dreadful anticipation after 9-11 had happened all over again. Newscasters repeated the fearsome synopsis: Every attempt at diplomacy had failed. Governments in Palestine, Lebanon, Iran, Somalia, Syria, Afghanistan, and Iraq had been seized or were controlled by political forces that sponsored terrorism throughout the world, declared their solidarity, and called for jihad against any non-Muslim who set foot on their sacred sands. Resident Christians and non-radical Muslims were rounded up and converted or beheaded by the thousands in the name of Wahhabism. Terror groups supported by al Qaeda, Hamas, and Hezbollah were financed by these Wahhabi Muslims throughout the Middle East and Africa. They formed "The Brotherhood," an alliance of all such radical sympathizers.

Wahhabism has its roots in Saudi Arabia and is at the heart of the ruthless form of Islam followed by radicals there. The indoctrination begins in schools and homes, where children are taught from infancy to hate all things Western and that their greatest aspiration is martyrdom. Essentially, in the name of Allah, youngsters are taught to hope and pray for death to all non-believers. In mosques and universities, Wahhabi clerics and imams teach that it is the sacred duty of Muslims to convert by the sword or kill all, including fellow Muslims, who do not believe in their strict form of monotheism. Non-believers, commonly known as infidels, are worthy only of death. In fact, to kill one earnsa lucky soul a first-class ticket to heaven.

Now, after years of patient planning and organizing, The Brotherhood's campaign to destroy the infidel had moved across the sea to "the Americas." After immigrating through porous borders for decades, a network of assimilated, aspiring martyrs, as depicted by the perfectly American enunciation of the tape's narrator, had infiltrated the underbelly of Texas and were preparing an attack. According to the talking heads on every channel, World War III had begun when we were attacked on September 11, 2001, and the United States' level of denial in the years before and since that second day of infamy was becoming, well, undeniable.

Francis, however, had other things on his mind as he showered and changed, then bounded down the steps to raid the refrigerator and wait for Summer.

Summer arrived wearing a strapless sundress with pink flowers and a pink bow. Her hair fell over her shoulders and softly billowed in the balmy afternoon breeze. After hugging Francis and commenting that he looked great, she suggested they go to the bench at the top of the dune behind Francis' house to talk. She took his hand, and they strolled through "Annie's Garden," turning toward the beach and up the wooden walkway. Rolling dune grasses waved in the westerly breezes. Sailboats, windsurfers, and powerboats dotted the sparkling sea, and a string of pelicans glided southward overhead. The beach was sprinkled with sunbathers.

Summer looked directly into Francis' eyes. "Francis, how are you doing? Last night you got struck by lightning!"

Francis just sat and looked out over the pristine waters and up at the cloudless sky. Then, looking down, he said softly, "You wouldn't believe me if I told you."

"Of course I would believe you. Just tell me what it was like."

"Calm and quiet."

"Really? That doesn't make sense."

He looked up and turned to her, "See, I told you, you wouldn't—"

"No, I'm sorry, go ahead. I won't interrupt."

"After I got knocked off my bike, I was lying on the grass, looking up at the sparks shooting out of the transformer. Then, just inches from my face, a black electrical wire dangled in front of my face. It seemed to speak to me— no, it *did* speak to me. The buzzing wire said, 'Listen.'

"In a dream the other night, a voice spoke to me, too. It came from the waves. And the voice from the waves said the same thing, 'Listen.' That voice also called me by name and told me not to be afraid. And you know, the strange thing is, getting hit by lightning was never scary, and it was painless. When it happened, everything moved in slow motion and seemed very clear."

"Are you sure you're okay?" Summer wondered whether Francis might be losing touch with reality.

Francis smiled and shook his head. "See? You don't believe me."

"I want to believe you, but don't you think getting hit by lightning might cause you to see or hear things, kind of like hallucinating or something?"

"Makes sense, I guess, but explain why it didn't hurt, and why I don't have any burns."

"Well, I can't. Maybe you're just lucky."

"I'll tell you this, Summer, I've felt weird since it happened, like I'm supposed to do something, only I don't know what it is."

Summer laughed. "I feel that way sometimes — usually when I'm about to get into trouble!"

When it was time for Summer's mom to return from shopping, they walked back to the house and waited in the yard where the lightning had struck. The wires and transformer had been repaired; the pole was charred but intact. Black burn marks crisscrossed the street, the curb, and the edge of the yard. Burned into the grass where Francis had lain the night before was the outline of a boy.

≋

Somehow Stuart had managed to clean his vomit to the point where it blended in with the putrid colors of the carpet and chair, but it still stunk badly. At first light, he heard Carl's '89 Buick pull into the driveway. Stuart instinctively crawled off the couch and reeled down the hall to his room, kicking beer cans that littered the den on the way and closing the door behind him.

The front door opened. "Amber!"

Usually, Carl was pretty laid-back. He appeared oblivious to Amber's wild encounters and ignored Stuart most of the time. But on the rare occasion that he called her or Stuart by name, it meant serious trouble.

"Amber! Stuart!" He was getting more and more angry.

Stuart's door burst open. He was face-down under the sheets. The sheets flew back. "Boy! What in the hell happened here? It looks like a war zone! Who destroyed my home?"

Stuart looked up at his stepdad with blood-red eyes and said flatly, "Homeys."

Now, Carl was close to berserk. "What? Make sense, boy!"

Fearlessly, without regard for the impending consequences, Stuart said, "A bunch of gangster-looking dudes came over and were

99

partying when I got home from surfing. Amber probably met them at the club she goes to—as if you ever wondered where she goes at night. So, homeys trashed your home—"

Instantly, Carl backhanded him in the face and then grabbed him by the collar. "Shut up, smart-ass! Now, where is your sister?"

His hung-over head reeled from the blow. As Carl shook him, Stuart mumbled, "I don't know. With the homeys, I guess."

Carl shook him a few more times for good measure, then shoved him back down on the bed. "Clean this mess!" he screamed, and stormed out of the room. After he ranted some more and kicked a half-finished can of beer, he retired to the den for a dose of TV therapy.

Later that afternoon, Stuart managed to get up and go to Amber's room. Everything was where she normally put it, which was everywhere. Her pink cell phone rested neatly in its cradle on her dresser.

Dear old stepfather was on the filthy La-Z-Boy, entranced with ESPN updates and completely unaware of the recent human spillage, the remnants of which blended nicely with the other stains from who knows what.

"Carl, we need to look for Amber." Stuart never called his stepdad by name, but Carl didn't seem to notice.

Not looking up from the TV, he replied, "She's a big girl. She's fine. I'll bet she's down at The Strip with friends."

"Those guys she was with? They acted like they owned the place."

"Let me worry about your sister. Why don't you run to McDonald's and pick up some food. Get your sister something, too, in case she comes home hungry. Here's a twenty—and bring back the change!"

But Stuart knew something was wrong. Ever since his mom died of cancer, his sister had run the house. And she was always accessible, even if she was out partying, waiting tables, or bartending. Amber never left without taking her cell phone or calling to check in.

Stuart swiped a picture of Amber off her vanity, a candid of the striking twenty-year-old with long blond hair and a bikini contest-winning figure. He bolted out the door to Beach Boulevard and Club 17, Amber's favorite hip-hop hangout. McDonald's would have to wait.

Stuart detoured a few blocks northward. He emerged on 21st Street, the main artery off the interstate leading into the resort. He passed the legendary Peabody's and the new club, Sharks, then worked his way through the crowds to Beachstreet and turned right onto the trolley lane, just missing three elderly men in plaid shorts, golf shirts, and knee-high black socks. The resort was packed. A homeless lady with a full shopping bag sat mumbling in the alcove of a closed pancake house. A preppy family of four, pastel sweaters tied neatly around shoulders and waists, window-shopped for souvenirs. A bikini-clad trio of loud and laughing twenty-somethings walked side by side, swinging their hips to an imaginary beat, purposefully catching the attention of a group of young black men brandishing a video camera.

Then, as he hung a right up The Boulevard toward the club district, Stuart glanced down at the gutter and saw what appeared to be a piece of paper with a picture of a naked girl on it. His jaw dropped. He slammed on the brakes and turned around to pick it up. A girl with bright red lipstick, a red thong, a tiny top, and a diamond-studded belly button came into focus. She seemed to dance off the page. It was Amber!

Sporting her familiar smile and flowing blond locks, she gestured with a finger, "Come here." The headline read EXCLUSIVE AND LIVE TONIGHT. There was no date or time. Through the thick haze of the night before, Stuart remembered talking with Amber's party pals about what big crowds Club 17 attracted. One of the rappers he'd toked with in the kitchen described how pretty girls in miniskirts roamed the beach and nearby strip. They were employed by a promotional company named Hot & Sexy Shows Limited, and their job was to hand out cards with pictures of mostly naked girls and directions for how to find them. Of course, their "exclusive" locale was Club 17.

Club 17 had fourteen civil, fire, and Virginia Alcohol and Beverage Control citations pending. Of course, the club also retained a civil rights lawyer from Washington, D.C., who cried discrimination at every turn and offered as evidence the inordinate scrutiny befalling his upstanding clients. Stuart knew none of this. What he did know was that his sister had her picture splashed all over the beach and was supposed to be there tonight. The sun in his eyes, he squinted, peered up the street, and stopped in front of the club. The brick walls were painted black and purple. Weathered posters cluttered the facade and nearby telephone pole. There was a fresh, large poster on the blacked-out door leading up to Club 17 and heaven. It was Amber, "LIVE AND EXCLUSIVE TONIGHT."

Stuart hopped on his pedals and sped over to the McDonald's on 21st to get Carl's order. After ordering the quarter pounder with cheese and the fries, he added, "and a cheeseburger with fries and a Diet Coke." It was what his sister would always order. By the time he got home it was getting dark. Carl was still propped in front of the TV. "What took you so long?" he grumbled.

"Carl, did you hear from Amber?"

"Stop bugging me about her!' he yelled.

"Shouldn't we call the police?"

"What's gotten into you, boy? She's fine—probably down south in Hatteras with her girlfriends!"

Stuart was silent.

Stuart was also done with Carl. He slapped the McDonald's bag on the cluttered kitchen counter and headed to his room. Then he picked up the phone. In a few hours Club 17 would open.

"Hello, Mrs. Constantinides. May I please speak with John?" Stuart asked politely. He didn't want to appear anything but calm.

"Yes, oikay. Yannie! Phone for you! Eees Stuart!"

John picked up. "What's up?"

"Man, something bad has happened," started Stuart.

"What?"

Stuart blurted, "Amber's missing. She's been gone since sometime last night. My stepdad doesn't care. I think she's in trouble."

John was annoyed at what sounded like nonsense. "Aw, she's okay. What makes you think something bad—"

Stuart interrupted, "Her picture's all over the beach! He clutched the "Hot and Sexy" ad in his hand. "Last night when I came home, there was a party going on. Carl was at work. I mean, this was a serious party! Amber was really wasted. So was I. I passed out, and when I woke up, everyone was gone, including her. She left her cell phone. She never leaves without her cell. And she hasn't called."

Now John pondered the possibilities, but he still thought Stuart was worried about nothing. So, he asked cynically, "You think maybe they slipped her something to knock her out? Maybe they slipped you something, too."

Stuart did not detect the cynicism. "Maybe…I don't know. All I know is, she's gone, and Carl doesn't care. You gotta help me find her, man."

John took a deep breath and figured he'd play along. "What do you want me to do?"

"We need to go down to Beach Boulevard tonight and go to the place where she goes—you know, Club 17."

This started sounding pretty interesting to John.

"Can you meet me there at ten?"

John knew he could sneak out, and the later the better. "Yeah, I can do it." Then he added, "When she comes home today, you'd better call me."

≋

Stuart got to Club 17 first. A long line stretched around the corner. On the street were about twenty of Virginia Beach's finest: a dozen or so on foot huddled across the street; three on horseback; two on beach-cruiser bikes; several more in marked police cars. As Stuart got off his bike and chained it to the rack next to a group of beat cops, John appeared and pulled up next to him. While John chained his bike, they both looked around, then at each other.

John noticed Stuart's puffy shiner. "What happened to you?"

Stuart had forgotten about his cheek and eye. "Carl smacked me this morning when he saw the wrecked house."

John sympathized with Stuart's plight at home. "That sucks, man. Sorry." Then he surveyed the scene on the street.

Aside from most of the cops, they noticed they were the only white guys around. They were also the only fourteen-year-olds.

Cautiously, the boys walked toward the entrance of the club, where three enormous, muscle-bound bouncers sported red short-sleeve shirts with H & SS, LTD on the pocket. On a barstool at the doorway sat a blond girl in a red mini and bikini top; she looked surprisingly like Amber. Her belly button glimmered in the evening lights.

As the boys approached, even John was nervous. Stuart walked up to the girl. The bouncers converged, blocking his path. "Can't come roun' here, boy," one of them said in a deep voice.

Stuart pulled the picture of his sister out of his pocket. "Sir, this is my sister. Is she here?"

"Yeah, sho," chuckled one of the behemoths as he pointed backwards in the direction of Amber's look-alike. "She right here."

All three burst into mocking laughter.

"Boy, can't you see we got a club here? Go home to mama and let yo sista 'lone. She jes come roun' when she wants. Don't need no thirty-dolla' cover."

Stuart hung his head.

"Hey, come here," interrupted a raspy voice from behind the bouncers. The bouncers parted.

"I know Amber. She my girl. Wha's up wid her?"

Stuart stepped nearer to his sister's look-alike. Up close, her eyes showed creases of age and struggle, her midriff hung over her mini-skirt, and her blond hair had dark roots. But she was close enough to "Hot and Sexy" to pull in overcharged males hoping for a party.

"Is she here?" asked Stuart anxiously.

"No. She out wid people."

"Who? What people?"

"People from up north. Say they rappers from New York. One with all the bling call his'sef Salik. 'While back, heard he roughed up a girl. They come here an' party the last few days. I hear 'em talk about a party on The Sho'."

"The show?"

"Eastern Shore, over 'd bridge."

"What?" Stuart was getting frustrated. The Eastern Shore was a million miles from his mind.

Then, an irritated John said, "Man, she's across the bay on the Eastern Shore."

"Across the bay? Chesapeake Bay? No way. What's she doing over there?"

One of the bouncers had been listening. "Salik and his boys be hangin' there an' she wit dem. I seen her rubbin' up to Salik. He come here last night. Word from d' club, he grab his niggas an' she go wit him."

"Where on The Shore?" asked Stuart.

As they talked, the crowd pushed closer to the doorway. The bouncer turned from the boys and pushed them back. "Chill or you ain't gettin' in. Five minutes an' we open. No white Tees, no shorts, no baggies, no tennis shoes," he explained to the line of hopeful patrons.

As if on cue, the gathering of police across the street began to spread to each corner of the block in groups of three. The mounties slowly loped in the direction of Club 17. Music began to pump from behind the doors.

"Hey, kid," whispered Amber's twin, "Nassawadox. They say somethin' 'bout Nassawadox."

The doors opened. The first fine patron of Club 17 pulled out a "fiddy." He got twenty back.

When the boys returned to their bikes, John asked, "What are you gonna do now?"

Stuart answered flatly, "Going to the Eastern Shore—Nassawadox. You comin'?"

John reacted to the absurd idea. "You've gotta be kidding. How do you suppose we're gonna do that?"

Stuart was determined. "You're driving," he answered quickly.

"What?"

"Well, you look old enough, first of all. And we'll take my stepdad's old beater. He'll be home from work by then, passed out from his breakfast beers."

"It's too crazy. Why don't you just call the cops?"

"No. Amber could be into something wrong. I don't want her to end up in jail. We gotta do this."

Stuart's plea seemed to turn John enough to get him thinking. He figured he could tell his mom he'd be gone all day surfing or something. And his dad would be sound asleep after a late night in the restaurant. Besides, John liked the notion of driving a car. "Sure, why not?" he said after a short pause, shaking his head as if not believing himself. But then he added, "Bring money for the toll—and Stu, you're buying me lunch!"

"Okay," said Stuart. His adrenaline flowed from the events of the last twenty-four hours as he formulated a plan. "If you see his car, just wait around the block for me to come out. If you don't see his car, don't let him see you when he drives up. Just hide around the corner."

"Okay, I'll be there. See you at dawn."

They rode their separate ways. Stuart pedaled especially fast. He held on to the hope that his sister would show up or call, but deep down, he knew she wouldn't. When Stuart arrived home, Carl was at 7-Eleven, and the house was still empty. Navigating debris, Stuart went to his room and closed the door. For the next eight hours, he lay awake wondering where in the hell Nassawadox and Amber were.

≋

Peter knocked on Anne's door.

"Peter? Come in."

He felt he had overstayed his visit. What began as a few weeks to see his son and catch up with old friends had turned into something he hadn't expected. His son had passed out in church and been struck by lightning, the surf was better than he had ever seen, the dream he'd had a few nights ago haunted him, and the world seemed to be falling into chaos. He opened Anne's door and walked toward her bed. He needed to talk.

"What is it?" she asked sleepily.

"My head is splitting. I can't sleep. Anne, I've been here two months. Why? To hang out with friends and get to know Francis better, I thought. But this is too strange, living here and all. I don't belong here. My life is far away now. I—"

Waking up, Anne interrupted, "Maybe you do belong here, Peter. This is your hometown. All your friends are here. Your son is here."

In a few years Francis would be off to college somewhere. Peter realized time was running out. "Anne, what's happening to our boy? Is something wrong with him? First he faints, then he gets struck by lightning and shows none of the effects, except that he's acting different. It's almost as if he's not a boy anymore."

"He's just growing up," replied Anne with motherly simplicity.

"No, I saw something in his eyes when he lay there smoldering in the front yard. He looked right at me, but he had this strange, blank expression on his face."

Peter needed to unload. "I had this dream about me and you on a boat dodging waterspouts. It's like they were pulling me—us—in. I couldn't escape them. They had faces. Horrible faces. There was this cabin, and a doorway. I can't stop thinking about it—and all this news about terrorists in Texas—I'm a nervous wreck. I need to get out of here and—"

Anne sat up. "Peter, stop. Why do you think you're not supposed to be here? Francis is your son. He loves you."

"I've been gone for ten years. How can I keep disappointing him?" Peter responded, feeling terribly conflicted and not even sure he was making sense. But to Anne, he was.

"He'd be more disappointed if you didn't visit." Then, a figure appeared in the doorway, outlined by the faint hallway light.

"Francis! What are you doing up?"

"I heard you talking. Don't worry about me. I'm fine, really."

With that, Francis smiled, turned, and went to his room.

Peter and Anne looked at each other quizzically.

Anne said, "Maybe you're right. Do you think lightning has an effect on people's personalities?"

"It must. I mean, it would have to be a life-changing experience. But he's acting like the parent, reassuring us. And he looks at me with those big eyes, almost like he's staring right through me. Doesn't he seem older to you?"

"Yes."

Peter continued, "Even before, ever since that time in church, he's been acting different. Haven't you noticed?"

"Yes, I—"

"And smoldering in the front yard, he was so calm. He almost seemed hypnotized by the live wires. Anyone else would have freaked out. It's the same look he has now."

"Do you think we should take him to a doctor—I mean a psychiatrist—to have him checked out?"

"Honey, I think that's a good idea," Peter concluded, noticing he had called her "honey."

Anne noticed too.

At daybreak the following morning, Francis waited for his parents to come downstairs. He sat at the table eating Cheerios one at a time until the last one floated by itself like a life raft in a white sea. By the time Anne came down, Francis was ready to leave.

"Mom, I'm going down to The Strip to meet some people. I'll see you later," he said with an air of purpose and determination that got his mother's attention.

"Francis, exactly who are 'some people'?"

"Mom, don't worry. I'll see you and Dad later." He headed toward the garage.

Anne followed him as he walked his bike out the back door and down the driveway. She lingered, watching him. He turned. "I know I've been acting different, and it's making you and Dad worried. I'll explain everything later. I promise."

Anne watched her son ride away into the morning haze. For the first time in his life, she did not know where he was going or what he was doing.

Francis rode straight to the resort, where the tallest and newest hotels stood overlooking the boardwalk and mostly deserted beach. Ambitious joggers passed him as he chained his bike. Then he paused and squinted into the orange morning sun that hugged the horizon. The sea was as calm as a lake, and the sky was cloudless. Resting his elbows on the railing, he tracked two pelicans as they glided by, floating effortlessly in the still air, the tips of their wings almost touching the water. Farther up the beach, he could see a herd of bottlenose dolphins frolicking, breaking the surface with their haphazard leaps and slashes. An elderly couple holding hands strolled along the shoreline.

Behind Francis, a distant rumble intruded into the serene moment. It became louder and louder until finally, blasting directly overhead, an F-18 fighter bolted out to sea, banking to the left. Another followed close behind, then two more. No longer holding hands, the elderly couple stopped strolling and looked upward as the jets, all on the same path, turned back toward shore farther up the beach. Francis held his ears until the roar became a distant rumble once again.

Stuart stayed awake all night, waiting for Carl to come home from work, drink his usual beers, and pass out drunk. Like clockwork, as first light appeared and birds chirped, the Buick pulled into the driveway. Every sound was distinct: the closing of the car door, his footsteps on the dirt front yard, the door opening, the refrigerator door closing, the popping of the first beer, and finally, the TV. A few minutes later there was another pop, then another, then a few more. Finally, Stuart heard the bedroom door shut. Within minutes, Pops would be passed out cold.

Already dressed, Stuart pushed back the covers. He went to his dresser and stuffed his pockets with the forty-seven dollars he had hidden in the back of his sock drawer. He then cracked open his door and tiptoed to his sister's room. Grabbing her fully charged cell phone off its cradle, he moved down the hallway to the kitchen. The TV blared in the den. He quietly opened the refrigerator and snatched a leftover burrito, devouring it in three bites. Carefully, making sure not to jingle them, he lifted the keys off the kitchen counter and held them tightly. Once outside, he looked around for John.

John was not there. What now? Sitting on the stoop with his head in his hands, Stuart decided he was going to make a go of it himself, figuring all he had to do was make it through the toll, then just drive straight to Nassawadox. He carefully opened the car door, got in, and turned the key. It started on the first try. Clumsily, he put it in drive and carefully exited the front yard. He made his way past the trailer park and prepared to turn onto the next quiet street. He started to turn, then heard a thump and a crash. Behind him, John sat in the gutter, his bike a twisted wreck!

Stuart slammed on the brakes and raked the gear column trying to find reverse. When it finally engaged, he forgot his foot was on the gas. The wheels squealed and skidded as he backed, full-speed, directly at his fallen friend! John rolled into the grass; the bumper grazed his shoulder. The car sped past him until Stuart stomped on the brake, but not before he'd hopped the curb and leveled a stop sign.

John got up on one knee; a hysterical Stuart flung open the door and ran to him. "You okay? I'm sorry, man! I can't drive—I don't know what I'm doing!"

"Yeah, I'm all right, you idiot ... just a nick." John sat on the curb, realizing he'd just had a close brush with death.

"This is crazy!" Stuart said. "What am I gonna tell Carl? You sure you're okay?"

John just sat quietly.

Stuart calmed down. "Maybe we should forget the whole thing. We can't drive all the way to the Eastern Shore. It's a stupid idea. And what are we gonna do when we get there?"

Recovering a little, John looked at Stuart and smiled ever so slightly. "You love your sister and want to find her, right?"

"Well, she's always been okay to me. I mean, she—"

John cut in impatiently, "Okay, got it. You love her." He paused for dramatic effect. "Here's what we're gonna do." He reached into his baggy pants pocket and pulled out the .38, just enough for Stuart to see.

"Whoa," gasped Stuart. "We're not shooting that thing at anybody, man. No way. Let's forget the whole—"

"Look, I've thought about this. We won't need to use the gun, but we'll have it in case we need to scare someone. Look, it's not load-ed." He flipped open the cylinder. "The shells are zipped in my other pocket. We'll go do some shooting after we find your sister."

The notion of a little target practice in the country intrigued Stu-art. "That'd be okay. I guess the Eastern Shore has lots of farms and open land, right?" Not wanting to kill John's enthusiasm, Stuart kept quiet about the gun he'd seen at the party.

John looked down at the twisted wreckage that had once been his means of transportation. "Leave the bike. Let's get out of here."

With that, John, walking with a slight limp, got in the driver's seat and steered in the direction of Birdneck Road. They headed east down to the beachfront, then turned northward, beyond Beachstreet and up Atlantic Avenue. Passing Nick's restaurant, they continued on through North Beach and around the bend up Shore Drive for several miles to the exit for the seventeen-mile Chesapeake Bay Bridge-Tunnel.

The sign said TOLLBOOTH AHEAD. Stuart dug in his pockets and found a five and a bunch of singles.

"How much is it?" he asked frantically.

"Says twelve dollars right there."

"Let's see … six, seven — "

"Forget it. I got a twenty," interrupted John as he navigated the toll barriers and stopped.

"Here you are, ma'am," he said to the elderly attendant.

The two boys looked straight ahead. "Here's your change, sir. Have a nice day." She smiled. John smiled. Stuart looked over and smiled, too — and they were off.

Once they were through the toll area and over the slight rise, the seventeen-mile-long span appeared, along with the wide expanse of open water. The boys hooted and hollered.

"Look, a destroyer," remarked John. The ship cruised through the channel ahead at high speed.

As the boys crossed the bay, cargo ships loaded with several thousand twenty-foot containers steamed eastward to parts unknown to deliver their merchandise: toys, apparel, electronics, furnishings, and anything else that could be packed into steel boxes. Others sat moored in the bay, buoyed by empty decks. They waited their turn to dock and load their cargoes at nearby Norfolk or Portsmouth Marine Terminals, located on opposite shores near the mouth of the Elizabeth River. The common sight of massive, rusting hulks anchored just off the coast of teeming bay-front beaches is part of the million-dollar vista along the western shores of the Chesapeake Bay. These monstrous ladies-in-waiting seemed to stand guard over the coastal sister cities of Norfolk and Virginia Beach.

The twin cities also share claim to the world's largest naval base. While predominantly situated in Norfolk's harbors, the base stretches down the bay-front into Virginia Beach, where the choicest property is occupied by barracks, officers' quarters, training facilities, and every manner of infrastructure supporting the coastal naval community. Nestled in Norfolk's protected harbors, on any given day, rests the bulk of the United States Atlantic fleet. Swift destroyers, guided-missile cruisers, nuclear powered and armed subs, supply ships, other support ships, and, of course, the gargantuan floating cities known as aircraft carriers, all await their turn at service overseas. When aircraft carrier groups, often consisting of more than 10,000 sailors and their steady paychecks, get "called out," the local economies of nearby cities deflate, especially nightclubs and taverns.

When a carrier group returns from deployment, the region rejoices. Waitresses and bartenders fill their pockets with cash. Tourism aside, the United States Navy is the economic engine that drives the bay-side metropolis once called Tidewater, now renamed by marketing geniuses, Hampton Roads.

"What's that?" asked Stuart, as the bridge narrowed and caution lights flashed.

"Uh, I think it's ... oh, yeah, the tunnel." They would cross directly under the destroyer as it passed over. John tried to look calm as they neared the black hole, slowing down to about thirty-five. In no time, cars stacked up behind. Then the beeping started, which added to John's quiet distress. He entered the darkness. Once in the tube, as locals call the underwater tunnel, the beeping echoed and became louder.

Stuart turned his head to see the line of cars behind. "I think you should speed up some!"

"Okay!" John was petrified. They were going twenty-five now. The beeping got worse.

"No, really, go faster."

But John couldn't speed up. All he managed was a death grip on the steering wheel. After what seemed like forever, Stuart cried, "Look, there's the end! Just drive to it fast!"

John floored it up the grade toward the daylight at the opening ahead. The speedometer read thirty-seven.

"Faster, man!"

"It's on the floor!"

Finally, they made it out. By the time they had regained speed and a little composure on level road, another tunnel appeared just ahead.

"Man, how many tunnels are there on this bridge?" John was sweating. His knuckles were white as he entered the second dark cave at twenty-five mph. Concentrating on getting through without crashing against the tile wall or running head-on into a tractor-trailer coming in the opposite direction, John was silent. When the trailer passed, air sucked from the tunnel and seemed to pull the Buick toward it. John gripped tightly and stared at the growing circle of daylight ahead. Finally, they were out.

Over the honking, Stuart reassured John as they emerged back into sunlight, pointing ahead. "I think this is the end, 'cause there's the other side."

Stuart gestured to the barren shoreline coming into view. In a few more minutes, they left the bridge and traversed the causeway that divides the marshy expanse known as Fisherman's Island. They had arrived on the Eastern Shore. The sign read FISHERMAN'S ISLAND NATIONAL WILDLIFE REFUGE. Once beyond the refuge, a sign read WELCOME TO NORTHAMPTON COUNTY: LAND OF HISTORY, HOSPITALITY, AND OPPORTUNITY FOR ALL.

The Eastern Shore of Virginia stretches about seventy miles from the northern mouth of the Chesapeake Bay, known as Cape Charles, to Salisbury, Maryland. Two counties, Northampton to the south and Accomack to the north, comprise the historic, rural peninsula. In 1608, an English ensign named Thomas Savage landed along its shores and was later granted a tract of land by Debedeavon, known as "The Laughing King" of the indigenous people we call Indians. Savage established the first white settlement on the Eastern Shore in what is now Savage's Neck in the bay-side town of Eastville. Of course, others came, like Captain John Smith who, according to legend, said in the same year, "Heaven and earth never agreed better to frame a place for man's habitation." Many set down roots, displacing the Indians and establishing tiny hamlets such as Birdsnest, Treherneville, and Weirwood.

The boys headed up Highway 13 in search of a gas station or store where they could ask directions to Nassawadox. Farmland and tree lines flanked both sides of the road. Old, abandoned hotels and semi-rehabbed houses with real estate signs also dotted the vista. Then, about eight miles past the refuge and just past the turn to Cape Charles, they spotted a tiny produce stand. Signs advertising POTATOES, MELONS, TOMATOES, PEACHES, PEARS, SWEET CORN, VIRGINIA PEANUTS, HAM, AND FIREWORKS enticed travelers going fifty-five mph to stop and take home a taste of the country. When the boys pulled in, there were no cars in the dusty lot. A short, thin, gray-haired black woman greeted them with a smile and said in a soft voice, "Mornin', boys."

"Mornin'," John answered. The boys wandered around checking out the fruit.

"You wont somethin'?" She wasn't used to seeing boys pull up to shop at her stand.

The boys looked at each other for a few seconds.

"Yo mama send you here?"

"We're looking for Nassawadox. Can you tell us where it is?" asked Stuart.

"Oh, you wants directions. It's jes up the road a spell. The signs'll tell you where." Then she paused and put her hands on her hips. "You boys ain't from roun' here. What you wont in Nassawadox?"

The boys looked at each other, then Stuart answered, "We're visiting family ... my sister. She's there."

The old woman asked with a suspicious tone, "Didn't she give you directions?" But she still thought these were good boys.

"Yes ma'am, but, uh, we lost them," lied Stuart.

She knew he was lying, but wanted to help them anyway. "Well, how you gonna get to her house if you ain't got directions?"

Then John broke in, "Okay, we didn't lose the directions. We never had any. We just know she's there, and we have to find her ... I mean, see her ... look, we think she's in trouble with some people. Can you help?"

"The truth shall set you free, hallelujah! My land, you younguns is into somethin', ain't you? If you think she's in trouble, why don't you go get the po'lice?"

Stuart hoped he could trust her, then replied earnestly, "No, we can't. She might be mixed up in something bad. I don't want her to go to jail."

"The old lady thought for a moment. I'll try to help you. But you boys be careful and don't get yo'sef in trouble, too. I know a tomato farmer in Nassawadox—gets my tomatoes from him sometimes— named Bernard, Bernard Turner. He know everybody in Nassawadox."

Stuart pulled out the picture of Amber from her dresser and showed it to the woman. "This is Amber, my sister."

"Oh, my! She a doll. Sweet Jesus! I'm gonna send a prayer straight to heaven for you boys and yo sister, blessed Miss Amber."

Then she paused and leaned toward them as if telling a big secret. "You in *God's* country, now," she said. "That's what peoples call it here, God's country. Be careful, and don't you boys forget now, hear?"

With that, she gave them directions to Bernard Farms.

≋

By the time the first sunbathers spread their towels and slathered on super-charged tanning lotion, Francis, dressed in a BEACHES ARE FOR LOVERS T-shirt, white baggy shorts, and flip-flops, was sitting a few yards from a lifeguard stand. The white-nosed, bronzed lifeguard was just settling in for a long, lazy day of being cool and occasionally whistling at tourists who swam too far out. Behind the guard, next to the concrete boardwalk, a beach rental attendant unstrapped umbrellas, beach chairs, and boogie boards. Francis just sat.

An hour passed, and soon the beach crawled with tourists who set up camp. Besides the milling tourists, everything was still. The absence of waves and wind made for an eerie quiet on this brilliant summer day. Every so often, the laughter of a small child would break the unusual silence. Francis remained frozen, until a beach ball rolled up and bounced off his knee. A little boy no older than four ran over to him and stood, waiting for Francis to hand him the ball.

Francis reached down, picked up the ball, walked over to the boy, who had his arms outstretched, and gently placed the ball in his hands. The child looked up at Francis and smiled. Then Francis leaned down and whispered to him, "I won't let you die." The words came out before he could think about them. The boy looked at Francis with a curious expression, frowned, then ran to his family a few yards away.

Francis' brain caught up. *What am I saying?* But he couldn't stop. He turned away from the water and looked in the direction of the mass of people. He said, just loud enough to be heard by the lifeguard, "I am told by a voice to tell you something, so listen."

The lifeguard turned and looked down at Francis from atop his stand just as Francis gazed up at him. The sun seemed brighter. A new boldness appeared. "Listen. This will sound strange to you. There will be death today." Francis pointed out to sea. "A voice is telling me this, and now I'm telling you."

The lifeguard leaned down and stared at Francis. "What in the heck was that, dude? What are you talking about?"

Francis' eyes pooled with tears. He remained standing. "I said, listen. Listen to what I'm telling you. People will die here today."

"That's messed up, dude. Where are your parents?"

Francis raised his voice. "That's not important now!"

The lifeguard fumbled for his radio and called the head guard on duty. "Sunnyside to base, Sunnyside to base. Come in, base."

"Miller here. Go ahead, Sunnyside."

"We got a problem over here, and it's not a lifeguard thing. I've got a kid—he needs a shrink or something. What do I do?"

"Say again?"

"A kid here is talking crazy, says people are going to die. What do I do?"

"You sure?"

"Yeah, I'm sure. This kid is messed up."

"Roger that. Sit tight. I'm just up the beach, be there in minute."

Francis then raised his voice for hundreds of lazy sunbathers to hear. "Buildings will fall today, and many people will die. Listen, everyone! This is what I am told."

People rolled over from their tanning positions and sat up. Attempting to hear, others stopped talking to each other. Some shook their heads, while others laughed and shouted at Francis. One obese man heckled as if he were watching a flubbed play at a New York Yankees game. "Shut up kid, you're messing up my vacation!"

The heckler's voice was drowned out by a four-wheel ATV as it skidded to a stop about ten yards away. A burly, over-baked lifeguard in his late twenties with white zinc on his lips and nose unsaddled and strutted over to the stand. As senior guard Rock Miller approached, the younger guard gestured the universal sign for "cuckoo," circling his index finger around his ear and pointing at Francis, who had sat back down.

"What's he doing that's so crazy?" asked Miller.

"He's saying that buildings are going to fall and people are going to die today. Some voice in his head tells him," replied the lifeguard, rolling his eyes.

Miller then walked over to Francis, who sat cross-legged looking out over the ocean. Miller crouched in front of Francis, his large, dark frame eclipsing the sun. "What's your name, kid?"

Francis gazed eastward. He did not answer.

"Kid, am I going to have to call the police?"

Francis looked straight at him and nodded, wide-eyed. "Yes, hurry!"

"You said something about people dying. Is that right, son?"

"Yes, today. And buildings will fall." Tears welled in Francis' eyes.

Sarcastically, Miller shot back, "And where might these buildings be?"

"Right in front of you."

"There?" asked Miller, pointing to the massive high-rise behind them.

"Yes," answered Francis. "Please listen. People in there are going to die. And it's happening today." He got up and started toward the building.

"Okay, that's it. You're not going anywhere." Miller stopped Francis, hooking him around the waist with one burly arm. "I'm calling this one in." He radioed the 2nd Precinct and said there was a boy talking about people dying and buildings falling. In minutes, police started to arrive. Within an hour, news crews reached the scene of a bomb scare at the resort.

≋

According to the old produce lady, Nassawadox was only fifteen miles up the road. The directions placed Bernard Farms about two miles off Highway 13 at a dead end on the bay. As they wove along country back roads, the boys passed dilapidated barns amidst acres of soybeans and vacant, once-majestic Victorian homes. A trailer park packed with migrant workers moving about abutted a small cinderblock market. Farther along, an old brick Methodist church with a graveyard next door displayed the sign REVEREND LANKFORD SIMPKNS PRESIDING, SUNDAY SERVICE 10 A.M.

Hundreds of acres of corn hemmed the road, making the boys feel as though they were trapped in a maze. Finally, they emerged from the claustrophobic corn into tomatoes, red and bright orange, as far as they could see on both sides of the road. The fields were dotted with stooped figures holding baskets. They were tomato pickers, almost every one Mexican. Come summer's end, before their work visas expired, many would travel back to their homeland with pockets full of money. Over the years, these migrants and their US citizen relatives had woven themselves into the culture and fabric of the Eastern Shore. While they had their own neighborhoods, churches, stores, and restaurants, they also mingled with townspeople in general stores, shops, and banks. They bought and sold real estate, and were recognized as a vital element of the Eastern Shore economy. They had, quite literally, become a part of the landscape.

As the boys drove toward the tree line, they noticed a large white house, partially hidden by two long rows of gigantic hedges separated by a crush-and-run driveway. A white sign above the mailbox said BERNARD in black letters. They paused, then crept toward the house. The driveway opened in front and encircled a grove of majestic conifers. John slowly pulled up behind an old blue Ford pickup and put the car in park. The boys got out and nervously approached the veranda of the Victorian mansion.

"Looks like he's home," whispered Stuart, knocking. John stood behind him as they waited for some man named Bernard to answer. Nobody answered. Stuart knocked again. Still no answer.

"Let's try around back," suggested John.

The immaculately landscaped backyard led down to a dock and a tricked-out twenty-eight-foot Grady White with twin Yamaha 250s.

Then, from behind, "Hey, what are you doing here?"

The boys turned. About twenty feet away, a skinny old man in overalls and a John Deere cap pointed a double-barreled shotgun at them. They froze.

"I said, what are you boys doing here?" The old man peered over the barrel.

"We're looking for a man named Bernard," answered Stuart, trembling.

"Well, you found him. Now what—"

John interrupted nervously, "An old lady back on the main road says she buys tomatoes from you, says you know everyone in Nassawadox. She told us you might be able to help us find somebody. My friend here, he needs to find his sister."

Bernard slowly lowered the gun barrel and rested it in his arms. "First, that old lady don't buy nothin' here. I give her tomatoes. She comes and picks what she wants. Second, I do know everybody in Nassawadox. Now, why do you want to find your sister? She in trouble?"

"I think so," answered Stuart. "She's been missing for two days. Here's her picture."

When Stuart reached into his pocket, Bernard raised the shotgun, and then, as Stuart revealed the photo, dropped it back down. "Here's a picture of her when she won a bikini contest."

The old man walked over. Stuart handed him the photo. "Whew-wee, she is quite a looker. Been missin' two days, huh? Where you boys from?"

"Virginia Beach," replied John quickly, not wanting Stuart to get into any long explanations.

Bernard wondered. A girl who looked like that would not go unnoticed. "Well, what makes you boys think she's all the way over here in Nassawadox?"

"People say she's with some dudes that have a crash-pad over here," answered Stuart.

"Crash-pad? What the hell is that?"

John interjected, "You know, a place where people hang out and party."

"Not many places to party roun' here, boys."

John continued, "They have a house over here. You'd probably know them because they look like rappers. You know, they wear big white T-shirts and a lot of jewelry."

"You can stop right now. 'Bout six months ago, them boys come here and buy this house off Seaside on Hogg Island Bay, the other side of 13. Boys paid half a million cash. We see these boys around some—five or six of 'em. The story is they come from New York and want to make some kind of record or somethin'. Guess they like the peace and quiet. But when they drive round, you can hear 'em before you see 'em, if you know what I mean. Thump, thump, thump—the whole road shakes." Bernard Turner did not like these northerners.

"How do we get there?" asked John.

"Now, boys, you fixin' to get yourselves in trouble. Why don't you let me call the sheriff and let him handle this?"

Stuart begged, "Sir, please don't do that. She's my only sister. She might be in some kind of trouble with these dudes. I don't want her to go to jail. I have to"—he looked at John—"we have to do this ourselves."

"Well, what are you gonna do if you find her? Just walk her out of there without any problem? I don't think so. You need a plan. You got one?"

"Well ... no." Stuart lowered his head.

John started, "We need to find out exactly what the situation is. We'll sneak up to the house and check it out. Then we'll make a plan."

The old man thought a moment. "Okay, I'll tell you where it is, but don't tell anyone you came here, 'cuz I don't know you."

As the boys were leaving, old man Bernard called out, "Hey, one of them boys is named Salik, if it helps any."

Stuart nodded as they got in the Buick. "Oh, it helps. Thanks."

It was mid-morning. They headed back to Highway 13 and across to Seaside Road, where Salik and his entourage had bought a house in the middle of nowhere, supposedly to make the next great hip-hop album.

Following Bernard's directions, they crossed over 13 and made their way north along Seaside. From there it was only a mile or so to the dirt road near Brownsville that Bernard had said would lead them to the house. They saw the road on their right and slowly passed by, looking for a place to park and plan some sort of strategy. They drove ahead a few hundred yards, doubled back, parked on the next overgrown road, then got out. Surveying the scene, they noticed the dirt road was bordered on the left by a tree line and on the right by an abandoned barn and untended field. To the left of the tree line was a cornfield that spread several hundred yards from Seaside back to the woods.

The day was hot and motionless, except for two turkey buzzards standing guard on the electrical poles that lined the empty street. "Okay, see that tree line over there along the road? Let's walk on the other side and work our way down as far as we can. If someone happens to drive by, we can hide behind the trees," explained John. "See where it bends? The house is probably back there somewhere."

They started out walking along Seaside, then turned quickly, and hugged the trees that separated the dirt road from the cornfield. Along the dirt road was a power line that disappeared as the road twisted around the bend out of view. The corn stalks were over six feet tall, offering cover. The boys crept to the backside of a wooded patch that completely shielded them from Seaside Road and civilization. Insects buzzed; small animals, unseen but heard, scurried underfoot; birds chirped, and large crows squawked overhead, heightening the boys' sense of alertness.

The boys followed the power line and overgrown road. They did not notice the no trespassing sign. A little farther on they were startled by a small whitetail deer that leaped across the path and disappeared into the dense woods. She roused several great white herons from a muddy green bog bordered by cattails and bulrushes. Along the fringes of the swamp, wild sunflowers buzzed with bumblebees. In the clearing straight ahead, they could see an expansive brick manor house with two black Escalades parked in front, probably the only Escalades south of Salisbury and north of the bridge-tunnel. This had to be it.

"What now, commando?" asked John sarcastically. "We can't just walk up to the door, knock, and ask if Amber's there."

Actually, that didn't seem like such a bad idea: just walk up like two lost kids and ask for directions. But thinking it through, Stuart realized that the occupants would likely recognize him from the party. So, it would have to be John playing dumb by himself while he waited in the woods. There were five or six of them, according to Bernard. One kid with a .38 against five or six rappers who probably had guns didn't seem like such good odds. For the moment, Stuart was out of ideas.

The boys hunkered down along the end of the trees like hunters waiting for their prey to move into the open, both aware, however, that any shooting would be suicide and their bodies would probably never be found.

≋

As gawkers, police, and beach attendants gravitated to the scene, Francis implored the senior lifeguard, "You have to believe me. People are going to die!"

By now, sunbathers had gotten up from their towels and chairs to edge their way closer to the show. Miller replied, "Kid, you need some help. And talking about buildings blowing up and people dying's gonna land you in jail. You know the cops are calling in the bomb squad?"

Pointing to the nearby high-rise, Francis raised his voice, "Everyone! Stay here! Do not go in that building! Please listen to me!"

"Kid, we ain't goin' in there. Don't worry," hollered one man, figuring, like many others, better safe than sorry. Soon, however, near pandemonium broke out.

First, an enormous lady screamed, "My babies are in there. I've got to get my babies." Struggling to her feet with the help of others in her group, she waddled in the general direction of the hotel, leading the charge of folks whose sunny vacation had suddenly turned into an emergency. People ran toward the hotel to alert their friends and families.

About this time, TV news crews pulled up in vans. Police cruisers screeched to a halt along Beachstreet and on the boardwalk. Uniformed cops appeared everywhere. Crowds gathered, attracted to the growing commotion. Over the next few minutes, Police Captain Wallace coordinated crowd-control measures. Chaplain O'Leary and prison psychiatrist Dr. Schmidt arrived and took turns speaking with the boy. Officers sealed off access to him, while reporters worked their way through the horde to get a closer look at the youngster who had caused such a ruckus.

Some reporters, recognizing that the palpable sense of terror made for great news, ran toward the hotel to interview folks as they exited with their children or escorted half-dressed, confused friends to safety. Then the bomb squad arrived with their dogs and awaited Captain Wallace's order to clear the building and search for a bomb the boy said wasn't there.

Wallace spoke into his shoulder-mounted radio, "Send in twenty armored officers. Clear every hotel room. Get everyone out of that building—all staff, management, reporters, everyone! Move fast. I want this done in fifteen minutes. Then we'll do a floor-by-floor search."

Francis overheard the orders and cried out, "Don't go in that building!"

Onlookers gasped. Captain Wallace walked over to the boy, pointed, and said sternly, "You are going to have to be quiet. If you incite this crowd further, other charges will be brought against you in addition to this bomb scare. One more outburst and I'll take you to the station and put you in a cell, which I should do now." But he didn't. Perhaps the boy could help find the bomb, or perhaps his parents would appear and help explain what in the heck was going on.

Francis sat in the bright sun, surrounded by police and a mob that radiated out from him in all directions. He looked down at the sand and sobbed while twenty officers in full protective gear rushed into the building. People cursed their unfair dilemma, wondering when this mess would be over so they could go back to their much-deserved and paid-for vacations. In the epicenter of the pressing throng, Francis could hardly breathe the stagnant air.

Then, off in the distance, came the faint thunder of two F-18s, which, in less than a minute, grew to a familiar ear-shattering scream. Instantaneously, the hurtling jets flew directly overhead, shifting attention away from a crazy kid and a bomb scare. Francis looked up, along with everyone on the beach, as the sound of freedom blasted from above and straight out to sea.

≋

On the other side of the bay, Stuart and John had waited over an hour. There was no movement at the house. The late-morning sun and relentless mosquitoes began to test the boys' patience.

"There's got to be a better plan than sitting here getting eaten alive," said Stuart, swatting another mosquito that had drawn blood from his arm.

"Look, man, if you want to get your sister and make it out of here, you better shut up and sit tight," retorted John, as he slapped at his neck. "These bastards are eating me, too, but we gotta wait for them to make some kind of move so we can see what we're dealing with. If a few of them leave on an errand or something, then our odds are much better. That would be a good time to move in and see if we can find your sister. Maybe we'll get a shot at snatching her."

"Okay, I guess you're right, but I don't know if—"

Just then the front door opened, and three black men uniformly dressed in white T-shirts and baggy jeans walked out and approached one of the Escalades. They looked around suspiciously before getting in and closing the doors. The boys lay flat on their bellies. The SUV breezed by not ten feet away, disappearing down the driveway and around the bend in a cloud of dust.

"Stuart," John said, "we gotta do this now. We'll probably never get a better chance. Bernard said that there were four or five... or was it five or six? Anyway, there's probably only a couple of dudes left in there. If they see us, act stupid and lost, okay? Let's go."

They moved in like they'd seen soldiers do in so many movies, whisking across the unkempt yard, hunched over, palms downward, glancing in all directions. They backed up to the side of the house and looked at each other. A few feet down the brick wall was a window; it was slightly ajar. The boys noticed the faint sound of a TV and a female voice. John motioned to Stuart not to move, then slowly leaned toward the window and turned his head to see what was happening inside.

What he saw surprised him: two young, dark-skinned women with scarves covering their heads sat eating in front of the TV. Then, from the doorway to the kitchen, Amber appeared. She walked over to the table where the other two women were and sat down.

John pulled his head away from the window and whispered, "She's in there with two other girls. Take a look, but be careful."

Stuart peered in and saw the three in the kitchen. His heart quickened. Amber seemed okay.

"Hey, John, why don't we just walk up to the door and ask for her. She doesn't look kidnapped or anything. They'll probably just invite us in and everything'll be cool."

"I don't know, man. Let's hang a little longer."

Occasionally, the boys heard laughter from inside the kitchen. They waited for some indication that Amber was in trouble or that it was cool to just knock on the door and play dumb.

After a while, Stuart said, "I have an idea. Maybe I could tell them I was looking to score some of that weed they had at the house... that I found out where they live from the club. What do you think of—?"

Then a loud, deep voice intervened. "You ladies ready for a ride and a little picnic on our boat? We goin' in jes a little while, so git yo stuff together. Amber, sweetheart, put on yo pretty little swimsuit. Girl, you know that little booty of yours makes me cra-zy!"

Stuart peeked in the window to see the dude known as Salik lean over and kiss Amber, grabbing her playfully by the hair. All the girls giggled as Salik did a little bump-and-grind dance.

John froze. "Hey, listen. Someone's coming," he whispered. The boys turned away from the window and flattened themselves against the side of the house. They peered around the corner to see the returning Escalade pull up to the front door. The posse got out and paused to chew the fat and have a smoke.

"Jamir, you think that little piece of ass gonna like it over there?" one said as he lit up.

Jamir answered, "Naw, man. She just gonna be one a' his little flavahs for a day. He say he wants a blond American girl, but he got all kinda ass, I'll bet."

The other added, "Yeah, Russian ass, French ass, Italian ass, Chinese ass...shoo', I'll bet he got every kinda ass they is."

The three chuckled. Then it was quiet.

"My niggas," Jamir started, "we gotta keep cool today. Roun' two o'clock, when we take her in the fast boat, she can't know nuttin' 'bout nuttin'. It's jes a picnic. We all laugh, smoke some trees, then we off to meet up wit' dat cargo ship. She never gonna know till she gettin' lifted on. Up till then, ain't nuttin' but a party." They all laughed.

"Hey, we down," said one.

"Yeah, it's all good," added the other. They finished their smoke and went inside the house, carrying what appeared to be groceries and beer.

Stuart could hardly contain himself. Amber was being duped into taking a boat ride that would rendezvous with some cargo ship to take her someplace, probably very far away.

"Stuart, we need help. This is really bad."

Stuart agreed, "Oh, man, it's insane. What're we gonna do?"

"Hey, man, how 'bout we go back to Bernard? He's got a boat. Maybe he can help us," ventured John.

"I don't know. That old man and his gun...pretty scary." The boys pondered their next move. Then, coming from the farm next door, a group of figures appeared. They walked along the tree line at the back of the property. It looked like there were a dozen or so, and they were heading right for the house. The boys ducked behind a row of bushes.

"Who are they?" whispered Stuart.

"Hell if I know."

They all had ruddy complexions, and most wore black bandannas. Their sweaty shirts were filthy and torn. If not for their weathered, semi-bearded faces, disheveled jeans, and raggedy attire, they might have passed for an athletic team.

"Tomato pickers?" whispered Stuart.

"Don't know ... shhhh!"

The group approached the rear of the property like shadows. They walked silently up to the house and fell out of view. A few seconds later, the boys heard a knock at the back door. John slowly stood up to peek in.

As John looked and listened, one dark figure, who seemed in charge of the group, walked in, just as Salik motioned to the three ladies to go into another room, which they did with serious swiftness. The two men embraced and patted each other on the back. They exchanged greetings in some language John had never heard.

"Salam alaikum, Habibi!" offered Salik.

"Alaikum salam," answered the dark, bearded visitor. "Was that our prize, Brother Salik?"

"Yes, Habibi. Do you think he will find her suitable?" He bowed slightly.

"She is what he ordered. Now, are you prepared to deliver her to the ship? She must not know until she is being transferred."

"We have everything planned perfectly, my brother. She gonna be laughin' all the way, havin' a party with me and my boys." Then Salik paused and added, "Now, you've seen the girl. How 'bout takin' care of me and my dawgs like we agreed, half now and half when she's safely on the ship."

The visitor replied bluntly, "I will pay you when the job is finished, not sooner." Then, he tried to add a little finesse. "My dear Brother Salik, you—"

Brother Salik blew. "Listen, bitch! You give me my Benjamins now!" Salik promptly produced a Glock from his baggies, raised it sideways over his head, and pointed it at the mysterious bearded man.

"You people come over here and set up shop. I might be a Muslim, but I ain't one of you! Now, gimme my money, or I'll pop a cap in yo' ass, and the girl goes home to her daddy, bru-thah!"

The bearded man put his hands out in front of him and eased toward the back door. "Okay, okay, rest, my brother. We have the money. You get half now." Then he turned, partially opened the door, and called, "Kamil!" He spoke in that strange language again. He received a brown bag from one of the gang and presented it to a fuming Salik, who snatched the bag, looked inside, and nodded. Salik put the gun back in his pocket, then grimaced and shook his head. "Why you gotta be that way, man? We had a deal, and now you try to play me. Then it gets, you know, personal."

The rugged man smiled. "We are just different. Brothers, yes, but different ... very different."

"Hey, whatever. I jes wanna get paid. The ship sails out the bay in a few hours. The boat is ready out back. Once we shove off, little princess'll be tight. We be out in the ocean and up on that ship in twenty minutes."

The Muslim nodded, bowed ever so slightly, and left with his dirty dozen the same way they had come, hugging the tree line bordering the back of the farm, and disappearing around the bend.

Both boys heard everything. Stuart checked Amber's cell. It was 11:20. He showed it to John, who looked down, strategizing. What wouldn't work, he thought, would be a confrontation at the manor house, were weapons might be stored and walls offered protection. In such a scenario, he envisioned casualties and a possible hostage situation. At sea, Salik and his gang would have their guard down. "We need Bernard and his boat, fast. He's our only hope," John said with certainty.

After hearing John's line of reasoning, Stuart agreed.

The boys snuck away from the house, then ran along the driveway and out to Seaside Road where the Buick was parked. They sped over to Franktown and crossed over Highway 13 to Wardtown

Road, Nassawadox Creek, and the house of crotchety old Bernard. At 60 mph on country roads it was like a thrill ride.

Arriving at Bernard's, they skidded to a stop, kicking up a cloud of dust that drifted toward the house. "Boys, what are you doin' back here?" grumbled the old man, this time unarmed, holding the front door.

Stuart, beside himself, began to tell the story; John filled in parts that Stuart skipped. Bernard found the tale fascinating. If these crazy boys were right, a bunch of kidnappers posing as hip-hop artists, and Arabs posing as tomato pickers, were right there in Nassawadox! Bernard's blood started to boil. He hadn't liked the looks of that crew the first time he'd laid eyes on them.

Shaking his head, he reached behind the door and raised double-barreled Bessie. "Okay, boys. I'll help you. And I got some friends. C'mon in while I raise 'em."

The boys followed him through the house and into a cramped office piled with books, papers, and boxes. On the cluttered desk was a CB radio. Bernard turned it on. First there was static, then Bernard turned a dial and started talking. "This is Bernard over here on the Nassawadox Creek. Any of you boys out there?"

More static. Bernard looked at the boys and smiled. "Cell phones don't work too good 'round here."

Then he continued the all-points bulletin. "Boys, come in. We got ourselves a situation over here. Come on in now."

More static... then a gravelly voice, "This is Melvin at Hungar's Creek."

"Melvin, yes. We got a bad situation here. There's a young girl. She's in trouble."

"What kind of trouble?"

"...kidnapped by some northerners and some Middle Easterners. I got two young boys here that have seen the whole thing. There's at least fifteen of 'em, maybe more. How fast can you get some boys together?"

Another gruff voice jumped in, "You mean, A-rabs?"

"Yessiree. In a few hours they gonna put her on a boat, seaside out of Hogg Island Bay, then meet up with some cargo ship headed for I-raq or somewhere, and she'll be gone."

"You're kiddin'," chimed in another.

"That's what the boys said. Some sheik ordered her up for his pleasure. And they got drugs and guns."

"Well, I got guns. Don't need the other," said Melvin.

"Look," Bernard continued, "I'll gas up, then meet you on the seaside of Cobb Island in an hour and a half. You boys over here on bay-side south of me are gonna have to hightail it if you're gonna get there in time. We gotta cut through Fisherman's Inlet and head up the channel through Mogothy and Mockhern Bays, then through Cobb Bay to Hogg Island. You boys over on seaside just wait for us. That boat's gonna come a flyin' out of Machipongo River like a bat outta' hell, an' we need to get to 'em 'fore they hit open water."

By now there was a convention on Bernard's CB frequency. Along with Melvin from Hungar's Creek, there were, among others, a farmer from Eastville, a clammer from Cherrystone Creek, a charter-boat captain from Wachapreague, and some kid with a skiff and an old nine-horse Evinrude from seaside Bells Neck. Like Bernard, they were all armed and dangerous.

For the moment, the crowd on the beach had calmed a bit. The captain raised his bullhorn and pleaded, "Everyone, please stay here on the beach for a little while longer. We are sending a unit into the building to make sure it's completely safe. Then you can return to your rooms. It is important that you wait here, and do not wander near the building during this process. I will alert you when you may return." Then he spoke into his shoulder radio, "Okay, lieutenant, everyone's evacuated. Send 'em in. If they find a device, radio me before doing anything." Then he added, "For some reason, I believe this kid. I don't think there's a bomb in there, but make sure every inch is clean before coming out."

"Yes, sir," answered the lieutenant. A dozen officers with full gear and dogs entered the hotel.

On the beach, despite the captain's update, the scene turned increasingly tense. By this time, hundreds of people had assembled; most were annoyed, and some plain angry, all waiting for the signal that this was all just a hoax. Arguments flared and officers intervened.

Then, in the back of the crowd near the boardwalk, there was a small commotion. A man began moving through. He was slender, gray, and unshaven, and seemed to know Captain Wallace, walking straight to him. They shook hands and exchanged a few words. Then, the captain patted the man on the back and let him by. With a slight smile and calm manner, he approached Francis, who sat, head bowed. When the man crouched down and touched his shoulder, Francis looked up.

The man peered into Francis' eyes. "You got everyone scared around here, boy. What's your name?"

"Not important."

The man looked even closer. "I know you. You were out there that surf day at Pendleton. You're Peter's kid."

"It doesn't matter," Francis replied, then bowed his head in his hands again.

Off in the distance, the two jets that had flown over just minutes before came back into view. One veered northward, the other headed due west. About two miles out, it dropped low to the water, causing a boom that shook the beach. Everyone turned. Francis looked up, wide-eyed, then, unable to watch, looked down and covered his ears. The jet kept coming, nearly skimming the water. People held their ears. Gasps erupted when, a few hundred yards out, the pilot ejected. Catapulting high over the hotel, his momentum launched him across the street.

Instantaneously, screaming by at 800 miles per hour, carrying a full munitions payload and 900 gallons of fuel, the twenty-five-ton F-18 jet-turned-missile disappeared into the center of the hotel as if slicing through a wheel of soft brie. The high-rise absorbed the plane for a millisecond, then the earth shook, and the whole world seemed to explode.

Volkswagen-sized projectiles shot out of the other side of the building and crashed onto the five-story retail center across the street. Mammoth chucks of concrete and metal vaulted into the air and spewed in all directions. Anyone within one hundred feet was incinerated or concussed to death by the super-hot blast. The street, shops, and nearby parking garage were ablaze; people on fire ran howling and flailing helplessly. Eardrums were shattered and internal organs bled out. Windows broke in every building for a quarter mile. Molten debris flew hundreds of feet in the air and rained down, hitting bystanders, setting them afire, or striking them dead in their tracks, including Dr. Schmidt. Then came the bloodcurdling screams, horrific wails from people who, just a short while before, were angry that their vacations had been interrupted. The fine hotel that took years to conceive was a leveled inferno. Steam appeared to rise from the searing-hot statue of Neptune.

As the F-18 struck, it also disappeared from Commander Conner Hagen's radar screen. He responded as trained, arming two AAM-RAMs, air-to-air medium-range missiles. Airborne over downtown Norfolk, twenty miles away from the resort, a new F-22 Raptor, lighter, sleeker, more powerful than the F-18, and flown by Air Force pilot Hagen, provided a protective air cap, as it is called, over the metro region. The friendly skies over most American major metropolitan areas are under heavy 24/7 surveillance by US Air Force pilots trained to respond to any unusual or unfriendly activity, also known as air-to-air threats. Hampton Roads, with its ports, ships, and densely populated areas, is no exception. There was no training, however, for what was happening at the oceanfront.

On the beach next to a prostrate Francis, the gray-haired man pulled himself up from the sand. The heat from the engulfed high-rise became unbearable. Sweat poured off him. "You okay, son?"

Francis struggled to his feet, only to stumble dizzily and drop to both knees. The man staggered, regained his balance as he had done so many times on a six-foot-long hunk of fiberglass and foam, and reached under the boy's arm to help him to his feet. He carried Francis to the water, where people who were on fire ran to extinguish themselves, agonizingly mixing saltwater with their charred flesh. Francis glanced around as panic-stricken tourists, some bloodied and some ablaze, rolled in the sand and surf. Police and lifeguards tackled some who did not have the presence of mind to drop and roll. Others, including Captain Wallace, who used his bullhorn, yelled for people to stay away from the hot debris strewn about the beach. As the thin, gray man and Francis reached the wet sand, the man, out of breath, asked, "Hey, Pete's son, what's your name?"

"Uh, Francis," answered the bewildered and terrified boy.

The water, feeling cooler than it ever had before, seemed to clear the man's head. "I saw Peter that day on the beach. He pointed you out to me."

Francis' head began to spin. Fading, he managed to respond, "Yeah, that was me. You're... you're... Pete Smith." Then he passed out in Smith's arms, just as a bloodied Chaplain O'Leary arrived and knelt on one knee in the wet sand.

Suddenly, the earth shook again and eardrums rang. More screams. Everyone looked back aghast. At the speed of sound, the other F-18, loaded with Sidewinder, Sparrow, Maverick, and Harpoon missiles, along with other bombs, rockets, and a full tank of fuel, streaked over North Beach, breaking windows in its path. In less than the blink of an eye, it flew directly past the steaming-hot statue of Neptune reigning over the ruins, trailed by two AAMRAMs and an F-22 three miles behind. This time, there was no ejection.

The fully fueled and armed plane and the two air-to-air missiles careened into the middle of the busy street simultaneously, commencing a flood of apocalyptic mayhem at around 25th Street. A surge of exploding flames instantly vaporized cars and pedestrians. Bustling shops, restaurants, and hotels on both sides of the street were engulfed, left pulverized and burning as the bomb-laden plane and two missiles spread destruction in all directions. Hurtling south down Beachstreet, demolishing everything and everyone in its path on both sides, the fireball splintered into clusters of metal and jet fuel, finally stopping eight blocks from first impact.

The first establishment to explode into smithereens was Dough Boy's Pizza, one of Amber's old employment haunts and, coincidentally, the very place where infamous World Trade Center suicide terrorist Mohammed Atta had allegedly enjoyed a pizza. Records show that in February 2001 Atta also opened a mailbox account at the post office right next door to the popular eatery. The revered martyr was documented not only to have had an affinity for pizza, but also for blond waitresses. If Amber was an object of his affection, she never knew it.

≋

Along the other shore, Stuart, John, and Bernard sped over the calm waters around the bend through Fisherman's Inlet, ignoring the no wake markers. A flock of several hundred Canada geese rose over the islands straight ahead. The wary fowl felt the tremor first, and then the crew heard the boom of the impact.

"Oh, my Lord!" hollered Bernard, as he slowed the boat and pointed southward. Twenty-five miles away, plumes of smoke could be seen rising on the clear blue day.

"What was that? Look at the smoke! That's a huge fire!" exclaimed Stuart.

"Explosion's probably more like it. That's not far from home, man. Maybe a plane crashed," deduced John.

Bernard stopped the boat. The three gazed at the confounding sight. As they drifted, seagulls flew overhead, seeming to look for a place to light. After a few moments, there was another tremor, which caused the birds to flinch as if a hunter had fired upon them. "There it is again! What the hell's goin' on over there?" More smoke rose.

There was silence. Then John said plainly, "I think it's war, man."

Bernard paused, shook his head, and looked away. "Maybe it is, son. Maybe it is."

Stuart implored, "We don't have time to stop. They're taking Amber in another hour or so. We gotta hurry!"

A paralyzed Bernard stared at the rising smoke.

Stuart screamed, "We gotta go!"

With that, Bernard nodded, "Okay. Hold on!" And he gunned the 500 horses northward around Skidmore Island and through Mogothy and Mockhern Bays, leaving untold death and destruction miles behind in their wake. They had a mission: to rescue a damsel in distress.

At the same time, leaving the mouth of the Elizabeth River was a Syrian-owned cargo ship with a crew of eleven bound for Turkey. Among its 4,000 or so twenty-foot metal containers was one loaded with paint pellets, courtesy of what counterterrorism insiders called the Virginia Jihad Network. Initially, the web involved a secret group who played paintball in backwoods areas as a training technique in preparation for global holy war. The group was run by the brotherhood, Lashkar-e-Taiba, which, according to the US, is an officially designated terror organization with connections in Pakistan and Afghanistan.

Realizing the efficacy of paintball war games as a training tool, Lashkar-e-Taiba's leadership had decided to finance its fledgling organization by selling paintball pellets to other terror groups like Hezbollah and al Qaeda, hence the container of paintballs headed for Turkey's loading docks. But even more precious cargo was to be loaded mid-sea.

Meanwhile, Salik and his gang prepared for their picnic. They loaded beer, champagne, sandwiches prepared by the two brunettes covered in scarves, and a bag of Mexican hooch. Oblivious, Amber was already getting primed, sipping Cristal champagne and smoking weed at the manor house with the other dudes in Salik's entourage. She wore a pink halter and see-through white shorts over Salik's favorite g-string bikini. On cue, a few of the fellows pulled themselves away from the pre-party with Amber to board the boat and start the bilge blower. Dockside, Salik barked orders. "My bruthas, travel light. We ain't gonna be long, jes a little picnic with the ladies."

They all chuckled as they loaded the boat. Salik jumped on and started the massive inboard engine of the ocean racer. The rumble alerted everyone inside the house that it was time to go. Amber, completely unaware that she'd be heading for Turkey in a few minutes, walked happily down to the dock with her newfound friends. As she confidently strutted to the boat, each man stopped for a second to behold her blond splendor.

"That's quite a boat you guys have here!" she giggled as she climbed aboard.

They whistled and hooted. Amber stopped, one foot on the dock and one on the step-down to the boat. Looking back, she winked and joked, "Come on, guys, give a girl a break!"

Salik leered lustfully. She was definitely worth the money, he thought, as opposed to the two "covered" girls, who were only there to serve and service their men and, at the moment, keep Amber's guard down. The two remaining dudes and the covered concubines hopped on, the last man casting off the ropes.

The boat party started with the pop of another bottle of Cristal, which prompted a round of hoorahs. Captain Salik tipped a glass as he cruised slowly toward the mouth of the Machipongo River and Hogg Island Bay, where he would gun it. Fifteen minutes after that, they would be alongside a huge cargo ship with a dangling harness.

Less than a mile away, screaming through Cobb Bay and approaching Hogg Island from the south, was the twenty-eight-foot Grady and three sailors who had decided that a war was on. As they entered Hog Island Bay, they saw a sight that none of them could quite believe. In the heat of the day, it looked like a mirage. Due west of Hogg Island was what might be described as an armada. Altogether, over 150 boats, from a dead-rise skiff to a sixty-foot Hatteras, had assembled to save an innocent girl from being shipped off to some sheik terrorist! Old Bernard's call to arms had assembled seafaring Shore boys from as far north as Wallops Island and Chincoteague.

"Whoa! All right! Yeah!" Stuart and John jumped around the deck, almost knocking each other overboard, and raised their fists in triumph, yelling as fourteen-year-olds do when they're about as happy as possible.

Bernard anxiously fumbled with the radio dial. He searched for the fishing frequency used in those parts. "Well, my oh my, boys, Bernard here! We got ourselves a little welcoming committee, now don't we? Over!"

There was brief static, then, "Bernard, where you been, old man? This is Drummond from Oyster Bay! We been waitin' for you to come round."

"This is Floyd from Wachapreague. I got a TV onboard here, and there's hell happenin' on the other side of the pond. All the news stations are sayin' two navy jets crashed into buildings and crowded streets, killin' hundreds of tourists and police. It's like Armageddon over there. They think it's terrorists."

"Hey, Captain Bernard, Floyd, and everybody, this is ol' Ricks... been tail-grabbin' you outta Cheriton. That's a 10-4. And it looks like we might have some more over here wantin' to kidnap a girl."

Bernard cut in, "Lord Jesus. That's what me and the boys here figured. Damn!" He pondered the insanity of the moment, and then decided, "There's not much we can do for them over there, but we can save this girl here. We got fast work to do."

Old Bernard began commanding the fleet of sailors. "Now, I know all you boys are carryin' some kinda arms, but we don't want no shootin', no sir. Got a young girl on board that boat. Now, boys, what we want here is blockin'! We'll hem 'em in against the shore. Now we gotta keep together, so follow me real close, and stay on your radios. Let's group as close as we can and break for Machipongo. Got no time to waste. Let's put a plug in that river! Okay, let's go!"

Along with the Grady, the boats merged into a mass resembling a phalanx, moving as one huge wave to where they thought Salik and his unsuspecting crew would emerge. As the armada approached the narrow mouth of the Machipongo River, perhaps 500 yards away, the fast boat appeared from behind the marsh grasses that protected the river's opening. Salik, not yet noticing the party crashers bearing down on him just a few hundred yards off his port bow, passed a joint down to the cabin to his obliterated boys and girls.

"Steady boys...twenty knots...stay together," assured Captain Bernard over the CB.

Salik raised his head from the smoke-filled cabin. He casually looked to his left. "What the—!" In disbelief, he hit the throttle, throwing everyone in the cabin on top of each other and onto the floor. The boat jumped out of the water and quickly reached sixty miles per hour.

The Eastern Shore fleet had most of the mouth blocked by the time Salik and his shocked crew left the marshy confines of the river channel for open water.

"Steady boys, stay together! Throw them wakes!" urged Captain Bernard.

"They gonna get through!" shouted one skipper.

The faster boats, most of them huge charter fishing boats packing over a thousand horsepower, gunned it, thereby throwing enormous wakes, in an effort to keep the fleeing boat from circumventing the blockade. The slower boats broke ranks from the deteriorating formation to try to intercept the outlaw vessel and run it into the shoals of the Machipongo basin.

Captain Salik recognized this ploy to run him aground. He veered hard to port, straight at the partially disbanded fleet.

"He's comin' right for us!" blared the captain of a fully rigged sixty-foot Hatteras. "If you got rigs, drop 'em! Drop your rigs now!"

The crew of the sixty-footer, as well as the crews of the other charter boats, scrambled to drop their outriggers. The distraction of this seemingly fruitless tactic, combined with the washing machine-like mixture of 150 wakes, caused Salik and his crew to take to the air. The airborne cigarette boat roared thunderously before landing hard on its stern, pitching and lurching, bow first, amidst five-foot swells that intermingled from all directions. The boat stalled; its cracked hull began taking on water. Salik lay draped over the dash. Blood oozed from the corner of his mouth, his neck broken by the impact.

The first of Salik's posse crawled out of the cabin, soaked, blood streaming down his face, waving his white T-shirt. Next, bloody and crying, the two covered girls exited, holding each other. Boats gathered around the crippled vessel to have a look.

Then a horn blew. Bernard, the boys, and the Grady made their way through and pulled up alongside the swamped boat. Stuart quickly climbed over the side and jumped onto the partially flooded vessel. He pushed past the two women who now used their scarves to cover their faces like veils, past Salik's corpse, and waded into the dark cabin. Amber was not there!

In waist-deep water, Stuart panicked. He looked around desperately, then reached with his hands and feet under the water. First, nothing. Then he felt something. It felt like a person. He lifted with all his might and saw, rising above the surface, the unmistakable face of the man who had offered him weed and eaten half his Dairy Queen chili dog! He was not breathing.

Frantic, Stuart pushed him aside and ducked underwater. Then, he saw her hair. It swayed like a sea anemone. She was pinned beneath one of the dudes, eyes closed! Pushing him off and grabbing his sister all in one swoop, he lifted her to the surface. "Amber!"

He slapped her, shook her. Nothing. Her lips were blue. Stuart, crying in overwhelming distress, tilted her head back and remembered the lifesaving CPR instruction he'd received in PE class at The Academy. Managing the presence of mind to check her airway, he began administering mouth-to-mouth. Over his shoulder, looking into the cabin, were John and Bernard, who watched helplessly. The old man looked down, shaking his head. Stuart continued desperately to try to revive Amber. He pounded her chest. Still nothing. She was limp in his arms, blood running down the side of her face. He kept breathing and pounding until the old man stepped into the water and pulled him off her. Stuart wouldn't stop fighting to breathe life into her. At last, helplessly, he let go. Amber was gone.

≋

Sirens wailed along the beachfront, the carnage and damage catastrophic. Smoke billowed and flames raged. The entire bomb squad and their dogs were in the building when the F-18 hit. All died instantly. The heat and force of the massive explosion killed bystanders in the neighboring park and on the boardwalk. No one could stand within 200 feet of the hellish blaze. But this was not the worst.

Six blocks south, where the second F-18 had hit, the attack produced many more casualties and greater devastation. The plane had belly-flopped at the speed of sound into the middle of a busy pedestrian and shopping zone. At the time of impact, folks had already heard the first explosion, seen the smoke, and stepped out of their shops and cars to see what had happened. The sidewalks were packed with gawking people. Before they could react, the second jet mowed them down in an expanding ball of fire and metal that kept going for blocks before running out of momentum. Demolished restaurants and shops on the west side of Beachstreet, as well as hotels on the east side, burned out of control.

Police, fire, rescue, and other emergency response teams from all neighboring Hampton Roads communities and beyond were called. The governor declared a state of emergency and summoned the National Guard. In just hours, hospitals were overwhelmed, and the nearby convention complex became a triage center. By day's end, the death toll was estimated at 1,000, with over 2,300 wounded. After a week, there would be 1,946 known dead, including F-18 Commander Omar Chandia, as well as 2,579 wounded and maimed, plus one missing—a pilot whose known name was Hassan Joseph and who, like Chandia, had flown US Navy jets for over fifteen years.

In the mayhem of the bombing, police had lost track of Francis. The gray-haired gentleman who'd carried him to the water's edge had also carried him to his car, dodging rescue vehicles and distraught motorists, and had driven him straight to the hospital. On the way, he called Peter, who had heard of the attacks and was already on his way to where he thought Francis was. Pete Smith reassured him, "Your boy is fine. He saved a lot people today; he's a real hero. I have him with me. We're headed to the hospital."

Peter and Anne were overjoyed that Francis was all right, except for a ruptured eardrum. The two Petes exchanged hurried greetings and updates on the bombings. Peter repeatedly thanked and hugged Pete Smith for taking care of his son. Then Pete Smith returned to the beach where, half a century ago, he had surfed his first waves and, later, taught so many that surfing was good for the soul. Now, he just wanted to save some lives.

The hospital had already received the first badly wounded victims from the resort, so they released Francis to make room for many more. It would be a long day at Beach General. Peter, Anne, and Francis drove home, which now seemed like a haven. Peter and Anne's relief at having their son home and safely in their care quickly changed when they pulled up to their house. Blocking the driveway were three black sedans with US Government tags. As the family parked along the curb and got out of the car, six men exited their vehicles and stood, waiting.

The one who appeared to be in charge flashed his Department of Defense badge. "Mr. and Mrs. Kahne, I am special agent Wilcox, and we are with the Central Intelligence Agency. I am here to speak with your son. Is this Francis?"

"Y– yes," stuttered Anne, looking down at Francis who stood next to her.

Peter interrupted, "What is this about, sir?" Very annoyed but still calm, he wanted to be polite to these six very official-looking suits.

"It's about your son and the bombings. We want to speak with him."

Peter was now just plain mad. "Look, we've all been through friggin' hell today. This town will never be the same. And my boy just got out of the hospital. So, why don't you just—"

"Sir, we have orders from high up to place your son in the custody of the United States Government."

"What?!" Peter yelled in disbelief. "For what reason?"

"Well, sir, he knew."

"Knew what?" Peter snapped. He knew nothing about his son's premonition.

Francis intervened, "Dad, Mom." He looked at both parents. "I knew something really bad was going to happen today."

Anne knelt in front of Francis. "Now, honey, you've had a traumatic day. We all have. You just don't know what—"

"Mom, I do know. I knew the building was going to explode, and I knew people were going to die. It's why I left this morning."

"Ma'am, we don't think your boy had anything to do with what happened today. We just want to talk to him, find out how or why he knew."

Anne cried, "You're not taking my boy away from me. I'm coming with you!"

"No, *we're* going with you. He's my son, too," stated Peter defiantly.

The six men looked at one another. The head honcho said, "Mr. and Mrs. Kahne, of course, we want to speak with each of you."

They gave the Kahnes time to grab necessities and were off, heading south, past the burning resort, to Camp Pendleton, where there was not only good surf on occasion, but war games and the interrogation of prisoners, or in this case, the interrogation of a child who evidently knew when attacks on America were coming.

≈

Bernard embraced the boy he had known only a few hours and ruefully motioned with his free hand to charter-boat skipper Jackson Belote, who was closest of the flotilla to the disabled vessel, to come aboard. Captain Belote and John escorted the three survivors onto the *High Roller,* then returned to help remove the bodies. Amber was moved onto a separate boat. Bernard instructed the crew to get her body ashore and deliver it to the first funeral home they got to. At about the same time, off in the distance, speeding down the Machipongo River out of Willis Wharf, came the police shore patrol.

As the boat approached, John looked over to Bernard. "There are more of them, you know." Stuart sat disconsolately on the transom. John continued, "We saw these other guys who looked like tomato pickers, but they weren't. They talked really weird. They paid him," pointing to Salik's body on the nearby boat, "a bag of money to take Amber to a ship. I think they're hiding behind the house in the woods or something."

Stuart looked over pitifully. "They killed my sister."

"We have to find them fast before they figure out what's happened," said Bernard.

The boat and two deputies pulled along side the Grady. "What the hell's goin' on here, Bernard?" asked one of the officers on board.

Then he saw the disabled boat. "And what's this?" Finally, he spotted Amber's body. "Oh, good Lord, what is all this?"

"Wendel, I know this looks pretty crazy and all," waving a hand toward the bodies and the survivors. "These here people tried to kidnap this poor girl. We intervened." He waved his arm around at the newly formed Eastern Shore Armada. "This boy's sister is lyin' dead there 'cuz they killed her tryin' to steal her away. And there's more of 'em. If we don't go after 'em now, they'll get away. And Wendel, they're hidin' right up your little river there."

"You boys just can't take the law into your own hands." This was a situation Wendel Briggs had never heard of—as far as he could tell, a couple hundred good-ol' boys had stopped a kidnapping on the high seas and left four people dead and three more apprehended. He didn't know what to do, but he had rules, and he was going to follow them. "Nosir. I will not have a bunch of vigilantes running around here. Nosir, I won't!"

Bernard hesitated, then exclaimed, "Then deputize us right here and now. We're United States citizens, damn it! Them boys," pointing in the general direction of the other suspected terrorists, "they ain't. These young men," pointing to Stuart and John, "tell me they've seen 'em, and they're posin' as tomato pickers!"

"Sorry, Bernard, I gotta call headquarters on this one." The officer picked up his radio.

"Go ahead, but there may be a bunch of these bastards. The boys saw a dozen or so. Could be more, right boys?"

Stuart looked up, sobbing.

John added, "We know where they are. You need our help. And he's right, there may be a whole bunch of them."

Wendel, radio in hand, thought for a moment, "Look, I'm callin' this in. This is a crime scene, and the law is the law." Then he paused, staring down at his radio. Several other boaters chimed in their disapproval. Briggs weighed the situation. He shook his head, then said, "I may lose my badge for this, but here's what I'm gonna do. Okay, you're all deputized." He waved his hand over the fleet of boats and crew, like a priest giving a blessing. Still in disbelief at what he was doing, he added, "Wait for my orders, and don't go shootin' yourselves, damn it all!"

Deputy Briggs backed away from the Grady and gunned the patrol boat to the mouth of the Machipongo, followed by Bernard and the fleet. They sped to the brick manor house.

Then, as the patrol boat and the Grady glided to the dock, the fleet close behind, a crop duster buzzed overhead and dropped below the trees behind the farm next door.

Bernard and everybody else looked up and tracked the plane.

"What the...?" exclaimed Bernard, watching it dip behind the trees, then rise up and bank hard left.

They tied up to the nearest cleat. John and Bernard disembarked. Stuart said mournfully, "You guys go ahead. I'll stay here."

"No way, man. You're coming with us." John put his arm around Stuart and tried lifting him.

"Get off me! Don't you get it? My sister's dead!"

Then the crop duster flew over again, this time dropping a load of chemicals behind the trees in the general area from where the fake tomato pickers had appeared. Gunfire rang. The duster dipped out of sight. Some of the boats veered northward up the river in the direction of the shots. Others with smaller vessels ran up the bank next to the Grady and jumped out, toting rifles and shotguns. John roused Stuart, and the boys hopped off the boat and ran in the direction of the shots to join the now amphibious assault team.

As they worked their way just beyond the trees, they encountered a sight the likes of which had not been seen on the Eastern Shore since the Civil War. From the west, off of Seaside Road and plowing through a cornfield, the cavalry, in the form of fifty or so pickup trucks and SUVs, blew past the manor house toward the hidden property behind the trees. From the south, naval assault forces, which included Bernard, armed with a 12-guage loaded with buckshot slugs, and John, with Nicholas' .38, stormed northward through dense woodland. From the east, the rest of the armada sat beached or anchored. Crews leapt off their vessels, slipping and sliding up the muddy shoreline in the direction of the battle.

When they finally reached the hidden clearing, Bernard and the boys could see five small cinderblock houses and a few old cars nestled against the back of a tomato field near some tall pines. The vehicles and structures were covered with chemicals from the crop duster. Rapid-fire shots from the houses peppered the lineup of pickups and SUVs. The cavalry, who had taken position in the middle of the field, returned fire. John grabbed the unarmed, despondent Stuart and pushed him behind a tree. Looking him square in the eyes, he said sharply, "Stay here."

John and Bernard worked their way along the edge of the field until they were about fifty yards from the nearest building, where they saw muzzle flashes coming from the two front windows. They inched closer from around the side. "Look, propane tank," Bernard whispered.

Around the back was the white, five-foot-tall tank that fed the house. Bernard shouldered Bessie and propped it against the side of a tree. He took aim. It was an easy shot. Boom! The back of the house exploded in a flash, leaving a gaping hole. Smoke poured out the windows.

For a moment, the shooting stopped. Then the door swung open, and three men spilled out in a billow of smoke and fire. One was aflame; he rolled to the ground flailing and screaming. The other two fell to their knees, coughing and gagging. The Eastern Shore militia watched silently. Suddenly, from one of the other remaining houses, a shot rang out along with cries of anguish, followed by another shot and more cries. Thinking the shots were directed at them, the brigade answered the volley. They peppered the cinderblock walls with everything they had.

One fellow, a Realtor from Eastville named Hobbs, who wore

a shirt and tie, shouted, "Stop! Stop shootin'! They ain't shootin' back."

Gradually, the gunfire subsided. The militia slowly lowered their weapons. After a brief pause, more muffled moans of despair were heard, then another shot … then silence.

The air, land, and sea battle of Machipongo ended when nearby Exmore police arrived in marked Ford Explorers, followed by Northampton County deputies in marked cruisers, all converging in a cloud of dust. Before they got the call to respond to the melee in Machipongo, they had been called to render assistance in the disaster that had occurred only an hour ago. Halfway across the bridge-tunnel, they turned around and sped back to The Shore to respond to what they were told was a "war or somethin'" in their own backyard.

By now, word of the bombings had spread throughout the Eastern Shore ranks. While accounts were vague, everyone thought the same thing: terrorists had attacked the Commonwealth of Virginia, and some of them had been holed up right under their noses in Machipongo!

"Boys, y'all stand back! I don't know what's goin' on here, but the law is in charge now!" exclaimed the officer, as he jumped out of the Explorer waving his arms and unholstering his sidearm.

"Ron," answered Bubba, a large middle-aged farmer from a few miles down the road who wore blue jeans and a plaid shirt cut off at his shoulders. "Think we got some terrorists over yonder in them buildin's. We came up on 'em and all hell broke loose." Then he added with a wry smile, "But I think them terrorists stopped shootin' now."

"Nobody here leaves! Nobody!" barked the officer now in charge. "Earl, start writin' down tags of every vehicle, and take down everybody's name!" He paused, then asked, "Now, what about terrorists?"

"Well, they *wuz* terrorists," added the man, now perched on the running board of his jacked-up Ford F-150. He pointed at the two bearded men on their knees and the charred remains of the third. A din of laughter, anger, and profanity rippled through the ranks.

"They sure ain't no Christians."

The officer in charge interrupted, "Okay, Charlie, you and me are checkin' them houses...or what's left of 'em." He was Officer Ronald Parksley, thirty-year veteran of the six-man and one-woman Exmore police force. His family had thrived on the Shore for over 300 years.

The two officers ran between the four-foot-tall rows of staked tomato plants. They ignored the two men who lay gagging on the ground and dove against the first house they came to, panting and sweating. Everyone watched in silence.

Parksley kicked open the door. "Police! Freeze!" There was silence.

"Charlie, get a look at this."

Officer Charles Hardy had never seen action before. The worst situation he had ever encountered in his six weeks on the force was issuing a "no trespass" notice to a city slicker from Norfolk who'd made the mistake of complaining a little too loudly about "home cooking" in a local business deal gone bad.

The room was dark, lit only by two small windows cut into the block and by daylight streaming through the bullet-riddled, wooden front door. The remains of a laptop computer lay in shambles on a simple wooden table in a corner of the room. Everything reeked of incense and gunpowder. Lying on individual rugs arranged in a line were three bearded men, each with an exit hole at the back of his head from a shot in the mouth. "Three dead here," radioed Parksley.

Each house door that was kicked open revealed the same: bloody corpses of bearded men with holes in their heads. As they left the last house, Hardy noticed something protruding from beneath a Persian-style rug in the far corner of the room. He walked over to the foot of a metal foldout bed and pulled the rug aside. There was a hatch. He carefully pulled it open. The first several steps were visible, then pitch darkness.

Hardy called to Parksley, "Ron, we got somethin' over here."

Parksley turned and approached the kneeling Hardy. On the table next to the bed lay a flashlight. Hardy turned it on and shined it down the steps. "Hey, looks like we got ourselves a basement here. I'm goin' down."

Hardy eased his way into the dank, musty space, followed by Parksley. The cinderblock wall next to the steps was splattered with vivid fluorescent colors. The floor was packed dirt. Shell casings were strewn about. As Hardy shined the light along the wall, the mélange of colors continued. Then he saw mattresses propped against a faraway rear wall. Moving the light across the room, strange objects came into view. Suddenly, the room was bright; Parksley stood wide-eyed next to a light switch.

"What on earth? They were havin' target practice down here—and war games. Look at these casings." He bent over to pick up a few. "They been playin' with paint guns, and these here shells are from live rounds."

Hardy walked behind an obstacle and hoisted a paint-pellet rifle that leaned against a pile of mattresses in the middle of the room, which now looked huge. Then he went to a bank of lockers against the wall and opened the doors in quick succession. Helmets, vests, paint guns, pistols, and rifles spilled onto the floor.

"They were trainin' for somethin'. Would you look at all this? Unbelievable, and right under our noses. Damn!" Hardy shook his head disgustedly.

Parksley walked toward the hatch and said, "Not anymore." Then he called to Hardy, still in disbelief, "Let's get out of here."

"Total of thirteen dead by my count, plus two with severe burns," Parksley said into his walkie-talkie as he and Hardy exited the last house. "And we got ourselves some kind of covert shooting range buried under this here house. We need to call in the big boys for this."

"The big boys" were already on their way.

The officers quickly cuffed the two men, casually manhandling them as they struggled to their feet, and rustled them across the tomato field. Every few steps, when one of the two would fall, the officers would jerk him up and push him forward, causing him to fall again. By the time the prisoners were crammed into the marked Explorer, they were soaked in sweat, dirt, and pieces of ripe tomato.

"Any of you boys hurt?" Parksley called out to the militia.

"Don't think so," answered someone.

"Nope, I think the Good Lord took care of us today," said another.

"Amen to that."

"Yessir, amen."

Around the bend and a cornfield away, a dozen deputized marines had stormed the vacant manor house. What they found puzzled them. Upstairs was a room with a bank of five interconnected computer monitors. Things were orderly. There was a king-sized bed with a zebra-striped comforter and throw pillows. On the floor was a small rug. A Koran rested on the bedside table along with a neat stack of two dozen fresh Mexican photo IDs called Matricula Consular cards, all forged. The cards are commonly honored in America as valid proof of identification for citizens of Mexico — or for the few impostors who want to do business, bank, and generally appear as if they are from south of the border.

The other four upstairs bedrooms were smaller. In each of the men's rooms, there were half-burnt incense candles and marijuana cigarettes, as well as various pornographic DVDs. The women's rooms held small beds and closets full of dull, unflattering clothes.

Downstairs, in a room adjacent to the den, there was a sixty-inch, flat-screen TV and four theater-style easy chairs with cup holders. When they turned on the TV and started the generic-looking video that was in the recorder, there appeared on the screen a segment of a speech given by Louis Farrakhan in a Chicago mosque proclaiming the start of a revolution of black freedom fighters and prisoners against white oppressors. Prison was where Salik had found his posse. Farrakhan named this fight against the white man after his personal newspaper, *The Final Call.*

Soon, men in unmarked black vehicles descended on the scene, stormed through the front door, and seized all the computers, cell phones, video cameras, CDs, DVDs, and literature on the premises. Local militiamen still rummaged through the house, but the men in dark suits flashed Department of Defense badges and escorted them all out. The house was now off-limits to civilians, even if they were deputized.

As Exmore police grappled with the unprecedented scene at the farm next door, more black sedans arrived with men in suits flashing badges. Some of these agents came from the National Counterterrorism Center in Langley, Virginia, while others hailed from CIA headquarters, also out of Langley. They swarmed the houses, took pictures, talked on Bluetooth phones, and punched information into hand-held computers. But they had been more than one step behind two boys and the mighty minions from the Eastern Shore, led by Bernard Turner.

10. Coming Home

Bᴇʀɴᴀʀᴅ ᴀɴᴅ ᴛʜᴇ ʙᴏʏs left the tomato field and headed toward the Machipongo River to board the Grady. Their destination was Nassawadox Creek. The electrifying trip that had taken an hour and a half at top speed earlier took much longer at normal cruising speed. Stuart lay in the cabin. Bernard and John stayed topside. Little was said as they rounded the southernmost point of The Shore and headed north along the coast.

Then, as they cruised across the quiet waters of the Chesapeake, Bernard said, "Son, you were right when you said we got ourselves a war. The thing is, I don't think us Americans got the stomach for it. I'll bet you that even after what happened here and over there," pointing back toward the plumes of smoke across the bay, "we still won't get it. We always want to blame ourselves for this stuff. And you know what else? I tell you, we've had it easy for a long time. Oceans can't protect us from this kind of business. I wonder how folks are gonna handle that?"

Then, as the red sun hung low over the bay, a strange sound came from the cabin below, like the trumpeting of the cavalry. John opened the hatch. There was Stuart, staring at Amber's pink phone, which sounded the obnoxious ring tone that he used to hate so much.

155

Now, he whimpered, "It's Carl. What do I do?"

John could only shake his head. "I don't know, man."

Stuart slowly lifted the phone. "Dad…" as John closed the hatch.

John looked behind at the frothy wake that marked their progress and eventually disappeared as if they had never been there. "Got a cell phone?" he asked Bernard.

≋

By nightfall, Peter and Anne were given individual quarters at Camp Pendleton; interrogators did not want them to sway one another's stories. The two were questioned in detail about Francis. The feds wanted to know who his friends were. What were his interests and hobbies? Who influenced him the most? Did he have a girlfriend? And, most important, how did he know that a building was going to be destroyed and people were going to die?

In the course of their questioning, they learned that Anne frequented the nearby Association for Research and Enlightenment (A.R.E.), the foundation dedicated to the legacy of prophet and healer Edgar Cayce. Reportedly, while in trancelike states, Cayce would diagnose unseen medical conditions and offer treatments. Readings and counsel had evolved into broader prophecies of the future, such as his acclaimed predictions of the stock market crash and World War II. Eventually, after Cayce's death, he was designated a psychic, ultimately disengaging his deeply Biblical and structured values, which, according to his colleagues, were the essence of his teachings and prognostications. Today, Cayce shows up in bookstores under "New Age" amid volumes on witchcraft, astrology, and UFO's, rather than religion, health, or psychology.

But to many who knew him, the truth of the matter was his visions and prophecies were far from psychic — they were gifts from God. Anne's interviewers knew little of this. What they did know was that "woo-woo" people talking "woo-woo" stuff hung out at A.R.E.;

to the feds, Francis' apparent prediction fell into just that category.

Ultimately, the flimsy association with A.R.E. and whatever phenomenon had influenced Francis went nowhere. Francis did his best to explain how he had known, or rather, how he was told, that the calamity was imminent. He described the strange sequence of events, starting with his vision in Summer's church, his dreams, his being struck by lightning, and the dangling power lines that spoke to him. None of it made sense to the inspectors, except for one, who delved deeper.

"Son, you said you fainted in church and had a vision. Is that right?"

"Yes, sir," Francis answered, brightening up a bit at the notion of someone understanding.

"Do you read the Bible?" he asked.

"No, but my girlfriend does, and the people in her church do," Francis answered, noticing he'd called Summer his girlfriend and hoping she wouldn't mind.

"So, you say a voice spoke to you. Do you think it was G—?" He stopped abruptly and rubbed his chin with his eyes closed. He went no further.

The inspector, a Christian himself, knew about the charismatic worship style of churches such as Summer's and their belief that prophetic and medical miracles described in the New Testament occur today at the hands of true believers. But he determined that none of his colleagues would comprehend this, even though he knew it was boilerplate doctrine in those circles. So, he decided to leave notions of divinely inspired prophesy alone, sparing Francis unending ridicule and scorn from a public who would never understand that a boy could possibly know the mind of God.

Nonetheless, the fruitless interrogation continued. Other investigators took their turn. After several more hours of Francis frustrating everyone, one agent asked, "Son, can you tell us what happened to the pilot who ejected?"

The first pilot had ejected and parachuted beyond the parking garage, landing in a bank parking lot. Eyewitnesses said he was immediately picked up by two men who helped him into a white sedan and drove north up Pacific Avenue. The sedan was found ten miles away, abandoned a few yards off Shore Drive in a dense wood.

"No, sir. I didn't even know the first pilot ejected until you told me," answered Francis politely.

Just two miles north of Pendleton, sirens rang into the night. The fires continued burning, casting an eerie glow over the resort. So intense was the heat, that firefighters could not get close enough to fight the blazes. Helicopters and planes flew over and dropped flame retardant. US Air Force F-22s patrolled with orders to shoot down any suspicious aircraft, including any with United States Navy markings.

The target of navy pilot Omar Chandia looked like what it was—the remnants of a holocaust. Dozens of cars that weren't melted by the rolling fireball were tangled, twisted, and burnt black. People in those cars had been incinerated, as were hundreds of pedestrians. If there were remains, they were monstrously charred, frozen in time. While buildings burned and smoldered into the night, federal agents raided the homes of Joseph and Chandia.

Despite the elaborate background checks instituted by the United States Armed Forces since September 11, 2001, tenured navy pilots such as Joseph and Chandia were not included. Each had an impeccable background and came from an affluent American family. Both had infiltrated the navy fifteen years before the fateful day when they would accomplish their mission, attaining, as do all navy and air force aviators, top-secret security clearance.

E-mails and computer hard drives revealed that the conspiracy had been timed to coincide with the disbanding of the terror cell on the Eastern Shore. Fortunately, Stuart, John, Bernard, and local armed forces were just in time to stop them before they left.

Joseph, it was learned, was to eject, parachute to safety, get picked up, and be escorted to another locale not revealed to him via e-mail.

Weeks later, investigators concluded that not only hadn't Joseph known where he was to be taken, but also that the Virginia Jihad Network needed pilots as much as martyrs. So, he survived to martyr another day. Crackerjack US Navy F-18 pilot and Islamic terrorist Hassan Joseph was never found.

Chandia was the lucky one—he got to die a martyr, and mate with seventy-two virgins in the afterlife.

The cargo ship *Arabian Princess* sailed to Turkey untouched, but carefully monitored by US authorities. And a million paint pellets, undetected by newly installed radiation screeners at Norfolk Marine Terminal, arrived safely at their final destination in Syria. The Virginia Jihad Network would receive cash payment for delivering the valuable training tools. What became clear in the investigation was that the Eastern Shore cell not only knew of the bombings and planned to vacate that very day, but were to do so only after they were assured that Amber was safely on the ship bound for Turkey and a powerful Syrian sheik. Thanks to two boys, the suspected mastermind, Sheik Youssef Abdullah bin Muttaqi al Mutawakil Mohammed, was now fleeing for his life as the second most wanted man in the world, his luxurious life in a palace with servants and concubines over.

As for Salik, he had been played for a fool by the promise of fast money and hip-hop stardom. His e-mails and other information disseminated from the manor house indicated that he'd known nothing about the bombings or the planned vacating of the Eastern Shore cell. His final payment for delivering Amber would have been a bullet to the head, along with the rest of the ex-cons turned righteous Muslims.

Club 17, the fine establishment where Amber had met Salik and his gang, had its liquor license revoked because of a dozen Department of Alcohol Beverage Control violations, three stabbings, five shootings, and over 100 police calls within eighteen months. A two-year investigation determined that most of the problems had occurred outside its doors; however, after local civic groups complained, city and state agencies managed to cooperate in bringing the charges. Nonetheless, following appeals and threats of crying racism to the press by the club's lawyers, the revocation was overturned. The owners of the hip-hop club were fined $500 for each liquor-law violation, and had their liquor license suspended for ninety days. On the ninety-first day, they sold the club and its ABC license for $700,000; the buyers reopened the club under the new name Club Phoenix, launching it with a huge block party—admission $50 a head.

≋

By midnight, after asking Francis, Anne, and Peter a battery of questions, investigators released them, each receiving the personal calling card of the chief investigator. It was determined that Francis' apparent prior knowledge of the bombings was, in all probability, coincidence. Nonetheless, on the chance that it wasn't, Francis was given a special business card with a hotline to the counterterrorism chief and was asked to inform him immediately should he have any more hunches.

Emotionally drained, worn out from a night of questioning, yet thankful that it was all over, the three headed home to the comfort of their oceanfront home. Peter's life back in San Diego awaited him. Anne had her yoga and gym classes and nights out with the girls. School was starting up soon; Francis would have ninth grade classes with Summer.

The next morning, a wide-awake Francis sat at the breakfast table. Peter shuffled by. He went straight to the front porch and grabbed the paper to read what he already knew.

"Hey there, buddy. Morning." Peter mumbled as he perused the daily.

"Hey, Dad," responded Francis, playing with his cereal.

Peter went back through the kitchen into the den, where he turned on the TV to watch the news reports. Fresh off the wires was the story of the raid on the Eastern Shore terror cell. Francis listened from the kitchen.

"We have reports from federal counterterrorism investigators out of Langley Virginia, that a terror cell on Virginia's Eastern Shore was assaulted by local farmers and boaters. It appears the terror cell was a part of the Virginia Jihad Network. In a bloody battle, fifteen terrorists died—most of them committed suicide before being apprehended. Five were apprehended and are now being held at Camp Pendleton National Guard base in Virginia Beach. One woman, Amber Hicks, was killed."

Francis jumped from his seat. "That's Stuart's sister!" He ran into the den in time to see Amber's inset photo, tastefully shown from the neck up.

The story continued, "Reports are coming in describing a heroic battle near the remote Eastern Shore town of Nassawadox. More than a hundred deputized boaters, a crop duster, and several dozen local militiamen converged in what appears to have been a near perfectly executed attack on a terrorist camp deep in the woods along the Machipongo River.

"The Machipongo runs east of Nassawadox, near the confluence of the Chesapeake Bay and Atlantic Ocean, just fifty miles north of Virginia Beach, where this week's terror attacks claimed hundreds, perhaps thousands of lives. This area is where Captain John Smith sowed the first seeds of our nation in 1607. Now, 400 years later, a new drama unfolds in this historic and picturesque region. In Virginia Beach, people mourn while buildings continue to smolder. Despite this great tragedy, we are left inspired and hopeful by reports of a spirited band of American civilians who discovered, engaged, and defeated a group of sophisticated terrorists.

"We have learned that a farmer, Bernard Turner, and two fourteen-year-old boys led the raid. The boys are John Constantinides and Stuart Hicks, both from Virginia Beach. Sadly, Amber Hicks,

Stuart's sister, died during their attempt to rescue her from her terrorist kidnappers. A band of brave Americans from Virginia's Eastern Shore—"

"Dad, I surf with those guys! They go to First Colony!" cried Francis as he pointed to the TV.

The story continued, "This was the second group of brave American civilians to rise up and strike a blow to terrorists. The first were the passengers of Flight 93 on September 11, 2001. They are all American heroes. Our deepest sympathies go out to the family and friends of Amber Hicks and to those who lost loved ones in the attacks.

"This just in: at three p.m. Eastern Standard Time, the president will address the nation from the Oval Office. And more news coming in from our correspondent in Virginia Beach..."

Francis dialed the phone. "Hey, John, this is Francis."

"You okay?" John asked. He and his family had been up all night, talking with relatives from Baltimore and calling employees who were wondering, since National Guard troops had blocked all arteries into the resort, when and if Nick's would reopen.

"Fine, I guess. How's Stuart?"

"I don't know. I'm worried about him. He's taking it real hard. I talked with him last night, and he said all his stepdad does is sit in that chair and watch the news."

"You all right?" asked Francis meekly.

"I guess so. A bunch of reporters are outside, but Dad doesn't want to talk to them. He says they twist the truth. To be honest, I don't want to talk to them either."

"You don't want to be on the news?"

"I'd probably say something I shouldn't, or, like Dad says, they'd make me look bad. Everything's sort of crazy over here. Dad came home, sat in front of the TV, and cried. The planes missed the restaurant, but he said he doesn't have terrorism insurance to cover his lost business. He thinks we may have to go bankrupt. It's really pitiful. Nick's was having its best year."

"Man, what are you gonna do?"

"I'm worried. If dad loses the restaurant, we could lose the house, too." Then John added resolutely, "So, I decided I would help him. But I haven't told him yet."

There was a long pause, during which the boys seemed to realize they were having their first deep conversation. Life had become complicated. Tragedy had smacked them in the face. Sacrifices were needed. They both knew it.

Then John asked, "Are you really okay, Francis?"

He saw Francis differently now, not just a pudgy little kid who went to his school and could surf. He'd heard the rumors of Francis sitting on the beach and somehow knowing about the bombings; John was unsure of how to talk with him.

Francis knew that any explanation would sound strange. But he felt John should hear it from him. "I'm okay. Things are different, though. I guess you heard about what happened."

"Yeah, I heard you knew the planes were coming ... sounds pretty spooky," John said, lightening things up.

"Well, not exactly," Francis added hesitantly. "I– I just knew something really bad was about to happen. It was like, God told me, or something."

"How? I don't get it."

"I had this strange thing happen to me in church with Summer, like a vision. I blacked out in front of everyone. When I woke up, the preacher was standing over me asking questions. They were praying and singing and crying, and some folks were talking this weird language. Summer said they were speaking in tongues. Anyway, in my vision I felt that God or Jesus or something was protecting me. The preacher asked if I knew Jesus. I said yes and everybody went nuts. Afterward, I had some dreams. Our house was burning, and a voice spoke to me from the waves. Then, I got hit by lightning and—"

"What? Hit by lightning? No way!"

"Yeah, it was right in front of my house after we surfed that perfect day at Pendleton. It hit the electrical wires and knocked me off my bike. Then the wires started going crazy, dangling over my head, hissing, and I was just lying there toasted in the front yard. I know this sounds weird, but the wire seemed to talk to me, too."

Francis wondered if he had said too much. It was a lot for anyone to hear.

John kept it simple. "Then what?"

"Then ambulances and fire trucks came. The paramedics took me to the hospital, and funny thing was, I was fine—no burns, nothing—so they released me. When I woke up yesterday, I knew I had to go to the park. I felt that something really bad was going to happen right there. It was like I was being pulled or led." There was an awkward silence. "Hey, John."

"Huh." Thinking none of it made sense, John had begun to check out of the conversation.

"We should go to Stuart's," suggested Francis.

John, still confused, offered, "Okay, I'll see if I can catch a ride with Dad when he gets up."

"See you later"

After pushing through a group of reporters and cameramen outside their house, John and Nicholas got in the car and drove to Stuart's. John called Stuart's number several times, but there was no answer. Francis and Peter had arrived a few minutes earlier to find cars and news trucks from everywhere staked out around the block. CNN, FOX News, MSNBC, BBC, and all the local affiliates were represented; a mob of reporters camped outside the front door, waiting for someone to come out. As Peter looked for a place to park, Francis dialed Stuart's home again. Still no answer.

John and Nicholas drove down Pacific Avenue. Helicopters and F-22s still patrolled over the smoking ruins. News crews were establishing bases of operations everywhere along the roadside and in hotel parking lots. Nicholas clutched the wheel, ground his teeth, and stared blankly at the road ahead. John looked around in amazement, occasionally glancing over at his dad to catch his gloomy expression. The world had come to know Virginia Beach in a way Nicholas had never imagined.

John turned to his father and blurted, "When you open Nick's again, I want to help—you know, work there. I could hawk people on the sidewalk, be the host, bus tables. It would save money, right?"

Nicholas turned to his son, his bloodshot eyes filled with tears of joy and sorrow. This was what he had wished for, to have his son next to him, with him. During the long months when John had drifted away, he prayed every night to have his son back in the restaurant where he belonged. Now, it seemed his prayers were answered.

"Yannie, you come beck! Oh, my boy, you, you wan' to work an'…" Nicholas hesitated, and his voice dropped. "No, you don' wan' to work with me. You just say that now. You feel bad an' wan' to help you papa. That is good son. I happy for that. You good boy like I always know. You bad, like a drive a car an' take a gun, but you good too. You wan' help you friend try save hees seester. You jes growing up now. No, you no work in restaurant. You work in school. Get good grades an' go good college. I take care of the restaurant."

There was a new determination and strength in Nicholas' voice as they arrived in Stuart's neighborhood and approached the crowd.

Peter and Francis waited for John and Nicholas in the front yard. They ignored the pack of reporters, each hungry for a scoop. The notion of a fourteen-year-old boy who'd lost his gorgeous sister in an attempt to free her from homegrown terrorists, and the fact that he and another kid had led an offensive against a terrorist sleeper cell in a tomato field on the Eastern Shore, and that of all of this had occurred within an hour's drive of the devastating attacks just a mile away, was just too juicy.

There were others camped in the dusty front yard, better dressed than the reporters, who were not reporters at all. They were scouts whose purpose was to present Stuart a contract and a fat check to appear as a special guest on national talk shows or be interviewed by tabloids. But as the boys and their fathers gathered, nobody knew who they were. The fathers, having never met, gingerly shook hands, and the boys awkwardly hugged.

"I've been calling all morning, but nobody answers," began John.

"Me too," added Francis.

Then Francis offered an idea. "They're all waiting for someone to come out, but we don't have to wait. Let's just walk through everyone and knock on the door. If they don't come, then we'll yell to Stuart through the door."

"Sounds good to me," Peter said.

"Me too," added Nicholas.

They worked their way through the crowd, drawing scowls and angry words as they passed. "Hey, who do you think you are? I've been here three hours. You can't just—"

John interrupted and pointed at the portly, middle-aged reporter, "No. Who do you think *you* are? We're friends of the family. Are you?"

"Well, no, but…"

Peter, the politician, added calmly, "Just let us through, sir. We're here to offer our condolences."

"Let 'em through," snapped another reporter. "Maybe we'll get a word from the boy if he comes to the door."

The sea of reporters parted. John rang the doorbell. No one came. Then he knocked. Still no one. He knocked again, louder. Still no answer. Then, he called out, "Stuart! Stuart! It's John and Francis! Hurry up, come to the door!"

One reporter cried, "Hey, that's the other kid, the one who drove with Stuart Hicks. It's John Constantinides! The reporters and cameramen pushed in. The door swung open. Stuart hustled them inside.

After they'd all hugged and cried a bit, Stuart said, "Listen, Carl's talked to them a couple of times, but they don't want to hear from him. And he got really pissed at me for taking his car—roughed me up a little. Now he's sulking in his bedroom. I don't know what to do."

Peter answered, "Well, why don't you talk to them, and you too, John. Both of you boys did a really brave thing, and they just want to tell the world your story."

"Yannie, you are good at talking to people. Tell them about what—"

Nicholas was interrupted by a loud knock at the door. They all looked at each other quizzically.

A gruff voice said, "Beach Police."

Peter motioned to Stuart to open the door. Stuart opened it slowly. The crowd buzzed. Four uniformed officers stood in the doorway, leaning their heads inside, looking past Stuart into the messy den. "We were called here because of a disturbance. Is everything okay?"

Stuart answered, seeing an unexpected opportunity, "Well, we need some crowd control." Then he added, "Maybe you could get these people out of my yard—"

"Wait a minute," interjected John. "I've got an idea."

Later, after conferring with the policemen, the three boys, Nicholas, and Peter were accompanied to their cars by the officers. As they drove past the dumbfounded reporters, escorted by two marked cruisers, Nicholas rolled down his window and shouted in his best English, "The boys will give you interviews at Nick's Steak and Seafood House on 37th Street in a half hour."

Then the motorcade proceeded to Nick's. Those with press passes were allowed past the checkpoints. Within thirty minutes, Nick's was packed with reporters who paid $5 for Nick's coffee and $5 for Mary's homemade baklava. No coffee and baklava, no admittance—and no interview.

A few thousand dollars later, with a carefully placed canvas banner bearing Nick's Steak and Seafood House hanging in the background, the boys gave interviews to newspapers and news stations all over the globe. In addition, representatives from numerous talk shows and tabloids offered the boys contracts. The most noteworthy deals were struck right there. All told, in just one day, the boys had interview and appearance contracts worth nearly $1 million, plus a book deal in the making. With Nicholas and Peter as the masterminds, they also started a worldwide relief campaign to raise money for the small businesses that were victims of the attacks.

When Peter and Francis returned home that evening, Anne was sitting on the porch with a glass of crisp Eastern Shore Chardonnay. Dim light shone from the half-open door. Peter and his son walked through the garden toward her. Exhausted, full of baklava and Coca-Cola, Francis kissed his mom on the cheek. She hugged him tightly, not wanting to let go of her boy. When they were done, Peter reached out his right hand. Francis took it. They both squeezed tightly and pulled together in a manly embrace. Then, Peter and Anne watched him enter into the faint glow of the foyer.

Before Francis could disappear up the steps, Peter swung the door widely and said, "Hey, son, you know I love you, don't you?"

Francis turned, smiled, and said, "I always have, Dad," and went to bed, knowing his father was leaving the next day.

Peter turned to Anne, hugged her, and shared a sip of her wine. They stood on the threshold and looked out over the garden. A breeze blew from the east, rustling the leaves of the majestic live oaks and swaying the limbs of the sea pines that shaded Annie's Garden, signaling the start of the late-summer swell. A new coolness filled the evening air, along with the distant hum of helicopters and the cry of sirens.

Peter turned, looked deeply into her eyes, smiled, and said, "Annie, what would you say if I told you I...?"

Lord, make me a channel of thy peace;
that where there is hatred, I may bring love;
that where there is wrong, I may bring the spirit of forgiveness;
that where there is discord, I may bring harmony;
that where there is error, I may bring truth;
that where there is doubt, I may bring faith;
that where there is despair, I may bring hope;
that where there are shadows, I may bring light;
that where there is sadness, I may bring joy.
Lord, grant that I may seek rather to comfort than to be comforted;
to understand, than to be understood;
to love, than to be loved.
For it is by self-forgetting that one finds.
It is by forgiving that one is forgiven.
It is by dying that one awakens to eternal life.
Amen.

– The Prayer of Saint Francis

Acknowledgments

I AM INDEBTED TO Deborah Seymour Taylor and the late Patty Masterson for their instruction and inspiration, which remain after many years.

I am also grateful to Pete Smith for his graciousness and warmth. He is truly a legend, now more than ever. May his legacy live on in the hearts of those who dream of surfing the perfect wave and pursuing their life's passion. A special thank you goes to another surf legend, Harry Heinke, as well as retired Unites States Navy pilot Commander John Naher, for sharing their insights and proofing scenes for their authenticity.

For their expertise, guidance, and feedback, the staff at Cypress House deserve acknowledgment, especially Cynthia Frank, Michael Brechner, and Stephanie Rosencrans. Also, to my friends at Sunny Day Guides, Clark Winslow and Tracie Shepherd, go my deep appreciation for their encouragement and direction.

More thanks go to those who read passages and offered critique, including Heather Marks, Lois Gallo, Jana Pearson, Stevie Araiza, Elaine Anninos, and most of all, my wife Stacy.